HOLIDAY HUNTING
A SHIFTER SEEKER NOVELLA

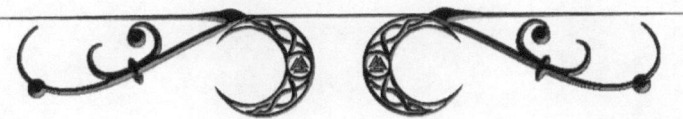

HOLIDAY HUNTING
A SHIFTER SEEKER NOVELLA

HEATHER MCCORKLE

COMPASS
PRESS

Holiday Hunting
A Shifter Seeker Novella

Copyright 2022 Heather McCorkle

Hardback ISBN: 978-1-939469-37-3
Paperback ISBN: 978-1-939469-11-3
eBook ISBN: 978-1-939469-12-0

Cover images from Thinkstock. Cover design by McCorkle Creations.

Second Edition, expanded.

Compass Press release date: 11/30/2024

AUTHOR'S NOTE:

Thank you so much for picking up my novella. This first half of this story was first published in an anthology. When I got the rights back I rewrote it, doubling it in size by adding all the material I had to cut for word count restraints required by the anthology. In essence, it is the same story, just a lot more of it. Two years later, I wrote a second story, Ayra's story, and added it as part two of Holiday Hunting.

This novella is a bridge story, bringing together the Children of Fenrir series and the Shifter Seeker series. It tells the story of what happened the winter between them. Can you start with this story and jump into the Shifter Seeker series? Absolutely, but I don't recommend it. If you haven't read the Children of Fenrir series, I highly recommend reading that first. It starts with an inexpensive teaser novella (free if you subscribe to my newsletter), Clawed & Cornered. A lot of world building occurs in the first novel that follows, Bitten & Beholden, and Holiday Hunting only brushes on those details, expecting that readers are carrying over from the first series and already know about the world. Will you still enjoy this novella if you jump into it first? I certainly hope so, but please keep in mind much comes before it.

POTENTIAL TRIGGERS

Some of the characters battle their inner demons in a fight that will end in madness, and subsequently their death, if they lose. Some physical fighting occurs as well. There is nudity, open door sexual content (completely consensual between both parties), forced shifting when an out of control werewolf is unable to shift back themselves, casual drinking of alcohol, a character dealing with the fallout of childhood mental and physical abuse, and paganism (worship of the Norse Gods and Goddesses, in this case). If you're still with me after all those warnings, I hope you enjoy the read.

THE CHILDREN OF FENRIR & THE SHIFTER SEEKER SERIES

RECOMMENDED READING ORDER:
Children of Fenrir Series:

Clawed & Cornered (novella)

Bitten & Beholden

Tempered & Turned

Bared & Betrayed

Shifter Seeker Series:

Holiday Hunting (novella)

Raven Rousting (novella)

Coyote Calling

Tiger Tracking

Bear Baiting (coming 2025)

OTHER BOOKS BY HEATHER McCORKLE:

THE CHANNELER SERIES (YOUNG ADULT):

The Secret of Spruce Knoll

Channeler's Choice

Rise of a Rector

To Ride a Puca

PART ONE

SONYA'S STORY

A nearly full moon held court in an indigo sky dotted with more stars than I could count in a lifetime. It pulled at me, that moon, drove me to trot faster through the frosty forest. My big paws helped me stay atop the six feet of snow that transformed the mountains of northern Montana into both something utterly beautiful, and deadly. Despite the fact the third week of December loomed just around the corner, I had no choice but to be out here.

More pulled at me than the moon this night.

The frantic pulse of a troubled newly bitten werewolf called to my power. They hadn't shifted yet, I could feel it. That was good. But, if I didn't get to them before the moon was full, their wolf side could take over and drive their human side insane, turning them into a mindless killer. As if things weren't bad enough with the snow and the waning night, their energy began pulling away from me. Soon it tingled at the edges of my reach— which I'd come to know was about a mile.

Head straight out, ears tucked against my skull, I ran with everything I had. Though I was much faster than when I'd been human, it was a sad comparison to most werewolves. Running had never really been my thing aside from a bit of jogging while I'd been in college. At least a nice crusty layer topped the snow, keeping my paws from breaking through and causing me to sink up to my belly. A second blessing of the snow was how it buried most of the underbrush that would have slowed me down even more.

Despite my efforts, in less than a hundred yards, the energy of the troubled disappeared. I cursed but it came out as a growl. Whispering a silent prayer to all the Norse Gods and a few of the Cherokee ones, I kept running. If I lost them now, I might never find them again. Moments later I felt the energy of the troubled one just ahead. Soon I caught a glimpse of a figure stumbling through the trees. Relief coursed through me. They tripped over something and fell face first into the snow.

The desire and intent to become human again set my atoms to vibrating and in moments I shifted, flowing from my wolf form as easy as pouring a beer into a glass. And that was where the graceful part ended because the moment I was human again, my feet plunged through the crusty layer of snow and I sank up to my knees. Being a werewolf meant cold didn't bother me much, but being naked and encased in snow still wasn't any fun.

Ignoring my misery as best I could, I trudged at top speed through the white stuff toward the figure. They weren't getting up. The sound of their ragged breathing made me feel a little better, but the sobbing did not.

"Hey, it's all right, I'm here to help you," I said.

They pushed themselves up out of the snow. It was a guy, somewhere in his early twenties. A short mess of dark hair clung in wet strands around a haggard face that might be handsome beneath all the dirt.

With practiced body positioning, I hid most of my nakedness with my long, black hair. To his credit, they guy didn't ogle me one bit. Though in a way that worried me. It might indicate how far down the rabbit hole of crazy he had slipped. But then, maybe I just wasn't his drink of choice. I clung to that, hoping it was the case.

"Right, sure, by putting me out of my misery," he said with a sniffle.

"Ugh. Why does everyone think that? I need a publicist or something," I muttered to myself as I walked closer. Louder, I said, "No. Whatever you've heard isn't true. I am here to help you make peace with your wolf side." I left out 'so when you shift for the first time you don't go crazy' because I thought that might tip him over the edge.

"I change my mind. I don't want to be a werewolf," he said through a sob.

My heart broke for him, but… "You did want to be, though? You consented to being bitten in?"

3

The guy's gaze zeroed in on me and he flinched as if I'd yelled. I remembered all too well how shocking the heightened senses were while going through the *verða*—becoming. "Yeah, but I didn't think it would be like this," he said.

"The overwhelming instincts, everything being heightened, I get it. It's a lot," I said in a soothing tone.

"I don't think I'll be able to control it," he said. Sitting in the snow, dressed only in a pair of jeans and a sweatshirt, he looked so fragile, so close to being broken that it pulled at the deep need in me to help.

"I thought the same thing at first too," I admitted.

At that he looked up from his lap and met my gaze. "You? The seeker chosen by the Gods, didn't think you could control your wolf?" He snorted. "Yeah right."

"It's true. I knew nothing about this life or werewolves before I was bitten."

He perked up a tiny bit at that. "Really?"

"Really. I'm Sonya. What's your name?"

"Dax." After a moment, he let out a long sigh. "This was not how I envisioned spending my holiday."

"Eh, it's pretty much how I imagined mine." Seeking wasn't exactly a profession that allowed for time off. The fallout of megalomaniacs biting in random people to wake up the power in myself and my counterpart—the reaper—meant a lot of people like Dax needed my help.

Scooting away a little, Dax looked up again. "Are you really the chosen of Odin?" he asked in a small voice.

"A lot of people think I'm chosen by Frigg and the reaper is chosen by Odin, but I don't know about all that," I said.

"So they're real," Dax whispered.

I gave a one shoulder shrug. "It seems that way. I haven't met them, but I have met a valkyrie."

Sitting up straighter, he looked at me like I'd grown another head. "No way."

"Way."

In a sort of wave-like motion dogs were so good at, he shook his entire body, starting with his head. Eyes narrowing beneath his dark brows, he finally looked at me as though he saw me. "You aren't cold?" As he said it, I realized he was shivering a bit.

"Not really, just slightly uncomfortable. One of the perks of being a full werewolf is a higher body temperature after your first shift."

His brows grew closer together. "But your standing naked in the snow."

I shrugged.

"Not even your feet are cold?" he asked.

"Nope."

The wrinkles between his brows eased. "That's kind of cool."

"It is. There are a lot of perks—heightened strength, speed, hearing, smell, longer lifespan…" I let my voice trail off, indicating the list was endless.

The guy shook his head. "I know, I know. But…" As he mimicked me trailing off, he looked skyward, toward the nearly full moon.

"But the moon is full two nights away and you're feeling the instincts of your wolf side amplified. It's freaky, I get it," I said.

I walked up to him and held my hand out. "Give me a chance to help you understand your wolf, and we'll go from there."

Gaze moving from my face to my hand, and back, he hesitated. Silence stretched between us thick as a banana daiquiri. Finally, he took my hand and let me pull him to his feet. I turned and started walking.

"Where are we going?" he asked.

"Somewhere with a fire."

At that he smiled and followed me toward his future. The tumultuous feel of his energy made me worry that it might not be the optimistic future I hoped for, but that didn't mean I was about to stop hoping. Holiday miracles could still happen.

2

Having been up all night talking, we slept through most of the next day. The crackling fire in our little cave helped. The smoky, sweet scent of burning fir logs combined with the popping sounds of the flames slowly devouring the fuel soothed both me and Dax. Every time he rolled over on the ground or even moved a limb in his sleep, my eyes popped open. I couldn't chance losing him. The full moon was tomorrow, which meant our time was running out and I couldn't waste any more of it tracking him down if he decided to bolt again. And I was not about to let a troubled slip into madness on my watch on the holiday.

Around noon when the heat of the fire on my toes relented, I woke and crawled from my sleeping bag. From my duffle I grabbed a pair of insulated yoga pants and a warm flannel. As I pulled them on, I listened for Dax. Soft snores came from the back of the cave in a steady rhythm.

It took a few long breathes blown onto the coals to get the flames to spring back to life. Once they began to eat at the wood I grabbed my phone. The flashing light on it told me I had a text, but I already knew that. The buzzing notification had awoken me just as much as the loss of heat from the dying fire. I unlocked my phone and clicked on my texts.

Ty: *How is everything going?*

My insides warmed just seeing his name. A few months ago him checking up on me would have irritated me to no end. But now I was glad for it. Too many people in our world knew about me and weren't exactly happy about my existence, so it felt good having someone looking out for me. I still valued my independence fiercely, which was part of why Ty wasn't out here with me. But being abducted changed a girl's outlook a wee bit.

Instead of texting him back, I clicked the call button. The holiday must be wearing my independent streak a bit thin. Rising, I walked from the cave to get a bit of privacy.

"Sonya," he said my name like a lover's caress, deep and slow enough to make my insides melt.

"Hey gorgeous, thanks for the clothes and supplies," I said.

"Of course."

"Things are going good so far. He seems open to listening," I said as I watched him sleep.

"Do you think he'll fight you tonight?"

It was always a strong possibility the night immediately before the full moon. "I don't think so," I said, remembering Dax on his knees in the snow, sobbing. Even if I thought he would, I wasn't about to say so. At the first hint of danger Ty would white knight over here and inadvertently interfere.

"I can be close just in case," he offered. Point proved.

Knowing it would not only drive him crazy if I refused, but make him suspicious of how safe I really was, I said, "Sure, but you cannot interfere until I tag you in. If he feels threatened I think he'll bolt."

"I promise I will stay downwind, out of sight, and will not interfere unless you call for me. He'll never know I was anywhere near," he promised.

"Please make sure he doesn't. He is skittish and I don't want him to feel threatened."

"I swear on Mjölnir."

The man took his gods and their weapons very seriously, so that was good enough for me. "Okay, chat tomorrow then," I said, voice dropping as Dax rolled over in his sleep.

"Tomorrow," Ty promised, sexy tone dancing all over my libido.

We ended the call at the same time. Sighing, I stuffed the phone into my back pocket and dug the camp stove and percolator out of the bag of supplies Ty had left in the cave for me. From an insulated cooler that was probably helping keep the food warmer so it didn't freeze solid, I took eggs and bacon. Minutes later I had a hearty breakfast scramble and coffee going that stirred Dax to life. By the time he returned from taking care of his morning necessities I had two plates overflowing with protein rich foods.

"Wow, is some of that for me?" Dax asked, hope heavy in his tone.

"Of course," I said as I handed him the bigger portion. More waited in a covered pan because I recalled all too well how ravenous the *verða* made a person.

While he literally wolfed his food down, I ate mine slow enough to take breathes and drinks of coffee between bites. In minutes he had licked his plate clean and turned big eyes toward my food. The desperate look on his face told me he might just be out of control enough to—

A growl tore from his lips as he leaned toward me. Lips curling back from my extending fangs, I let out a ferocious sound that made him shake his head, drop the plate, and scoot back so fast he fell backwards off the rock he sat on.

"I'm sorry, I'm sorry!" he said, hands held up to show he wasn't a threat, despite the fact he very much was, whether he knew it or not. "I didn't mean to do that…I just… Oh man, I'm so embarrassed." He buried his head in his hands.

Setting my own plate aside, I picked his up, dusted it off, and carried it over to the pan of leftovers. I filled it to overflowing and returned to where Dax sat on the cave floor. Plate in one hand, I held my other out to him. He stared at my open palm like it was something foreign, like no one had ever offered him a hand up.

"It's okay. You slipped, but you didn't lose control. That's a good sign," I told him.

Some of the shame melted from his expression. He accepted my hand. After helping him up, I gave him the plate. "Plus, you're literally starving because your body is burning fuel in overtime as it works through the *verða.*"

I motioned to the rock, then returned to my own seat and the remainder of my breakfast.

"They say you're a doctor, right?" he asked as he sat.

A sarcastic laugh slid from me. "The rumors about me are greatly exaggerated. I changed majors to psychology, but then had to drop out because, well…seeking."

"Oh. Well, do you know what's happening? To my body, I mean," he asked, fork poised over the plate.

As he ate, I delved into an explanation. "My best educated guess is that your dormant wolf genes were

11

awakened by being bitten in, and the atoms in your body are rearranging themselves accordingly."

He listened raptly as he ate, but didn't slow until he'd consumed half his plate.

"That takes a lot of fuel," I said, pointing to the remainder of food with an encouraging nod. Finished with my own, I set it aside and picked up my rapidly cooling coffee.

We sat in silence for a few moments as he cleaned his plate and I drank my magic liquid. When he finished he picked up my plate and carried it over to the camping table I had set up near the wall of the cave.

"Thank you for breakfast," he said as he turned back to me. "What's next?"

A grin spread across my face. "Next we talk about instincts, the reasons for them, and how understanding the reasons can help you think through them."

The eager look on his face gave me hope that maybe tonight—the night of his first shift, whether he wanted it or not—wouldn't be a complete disaster.

3

Contrary to horror movies, this time of year the moon started to rise in the afternoon, not at night. Which meant we had less time than I wanted. But after hours of great conversation in which Dax not only listened, but participated animatedly, my optimism had only grown.

The moment I felt the pull of the moon sliding up the horizon, though, everything changed.

The pale orb loomed huge and ominous as it lit up the snowy landscape. Though it wouldn't be full until tomorrow, it looked it to the eyes of a newbie wolf. And much like the way a cut didn't hurt until blood appeared, the sight of the moon stirred the anxiety in Dax like a hornet's nest. His power buzzed with it enough to almost sting me from several feet away. His heartbeat increased to a rhythm worthy of Viking battle drums. The sound became nearly deafening to me, which meant it had to be a hundred times worse for him. Panting as if he'd just run a marathon, he shot to his feet. Eyes opening wide, his gaze flicked about the cave. The tension in both his muscles and power told me he was about to bolt.

"Easy there," I whispered, needing to distract him but not wanting to add to the cacophony of sounds reverberating about inside his head.

He pulled his jacket out and began trying to fan himself with it. "Why is it suddenly so hot?"

"Remember what I said about your atoms vibrating in preparation for shifting?" I said gently, trying to ease some of his anxiety with my calm tone.

Swallowing hard, he nodded.

"That's what you're feeling. It's perfectly normal. Now would be a good time to take any clothes off you don't want to ruin."

Eyes going impossibly wider, he shook his head. "No. Nope. I'm not ready for this." The desperation in his tone shot a spike of concern through me.

"You are ready. You've got this," I assured him.

He began to shake, or vibrate, rather. A small whine slid between his pursed lips.

"It's okay to be afraid. Just know that I'm here with you and I won't let anything bad happen," I said. Having every intention of ensuring that helped me sound convincing, even if I didn't fully believe it myself.

The whine issuing from him only intensified. Maybe I didn't sound as convincing as I thought. From the snow-laden pine tree to the left of the cave came an encouraging bird noise. I searched for the sound, finally spotting a huge black bird high in the tree. Crazy thing must have missed the migration train.

Though Dax laughed, tension still sang through his power. He took his jacket off, followed quickly by his shirt and shoes. Hand hovering over the button of his jeans, his wide eyes fixed on me. Realizing he was having a moment of shyness, I turned slightly away.

"Don't worry, you'll be covered in fur in a moment and I won't be able to see a thing," I reassured him.

A blur of dark hair and blue jeans shot past me like a bolt loosed from a bow. Apparently that had been the exact wrong thing to say.

"Dammit!" I cursed as I tore my own clothes off and tossed them deep enough into the cave they hopefully wouldn't get covered in snow. Great, now he wouldn't have any clothes because shifting would rip them to shreds. And with the moon full tomorrow, shifting was a certainty for him, not an option.

Since I took the time to strip, he got a good head start on me. Thankfully with Dax's trail in the snow, he wasn't hard to track. Cold air kissed my skin for only a fraction of a second before I shifted into wolf form and hit the ground on all fours running. Dax didn't even make it to the treeline before the urge to shift became too strong for him to fight. Little bits of clothing exploded into the night like confetti around him. His image blurred as it flowed from man to wolf—a big grey and brown one. As soon as it solidified, he took off like a rocket.

I tried to curse, but it came out as a growl.

Being unfamiliar with his wolf form, I'd hoped he'd be clumsy, or at the very least sink into the snow deep enough to slow him down. No such luck. Propelled by inhuman speed, he glided across the top of the frozen landscape. Dammit. Why did it seem like I was the only clumsy werewolf in existence?

Kicking it into high gear, I gave chase. This was going to be a long night.

After what felt like an eternity of running, I caught up to Dax deep into the forest. He stood at the bottom of a tree, front paws as high as he could reach on the rough bark, snarling for all he was worth up into the fir boughs. At the top perched another huge black bird. Or was it the same one? I couldn't tell. It didn't matter. What did, was that it had distracted Dax long enough to make him stop and allow me to catch up. For that, I was grateful. I shifted to human form. The warmth of my nearly waist length hair was all I needed after running for hours after this guy.

"Wolves can't climb, Dax. You want that bird, you're going to have to shift back into a human," I told him.

Fangs bared, he whipped around and snarled at me. His eyes glowed, not just the shine of a predator, but the with the power of a shifter. In them I couldn't find his rational human side. That look said he hadn't understood a word I said. Not a good sign.

The snarl turned into a full-on growl.

"Your name is Dax. You love holiday music, video games, and the idea of Santa Claus," I began.

His quivering lips started to lower, covering his fangs a bit. I took it as a good sign.

"You want to get your first Yule tree, to make friends to buy presents for, find a family. Come back and you will have all of those things. Come back, Dax," I continued.

The hair along his spine began to lay down. I saw his human side in his eyes. Then the Lokidammed bird called from somewhere up in the tree.

Teeth gnashing, Dax lunged at me like a predator protecting his prey. I dodged. He plunged face first into the snow. Unfortunately, my foot broke through the icy top layer, toppling me over. My hand sank, followed by my entire body. I shifted back to wolf form, using all four legs to spring up and free myself. Before I could recover completely, Dax leaped for me. Jaws snapped close to my shoulder. I swiped a paw at him with all my might. The strike connected with the side of his face and sent him sprawling.

We danced a messy dance of swiping and snapping at one another. The snow soon packed down due to our struggles. As he tired, he began to fight harder, his moves developing a desperation to them that quickly grew even more dangerous. Sharp fangs came all too close to my neck more than once. I'd been trying not to hurt him, but I wouldn't be able to keep it up much longer. The last thing I wanted was for him to have to spend the holiday in the shifter hospital in Hemlock Hollow. But I didn't want to end up there myself either.

If I didn't want to hurt him, or let him hurt me, it left me only one option.

I turned and ran.

Like I planned, he caught up to me just outside the cave we'd taken shelter in the day before. I shifted to human form. The abrupt change made Dax shake his lupine head and draw back a step. Another bad sign among many. It meant his mind couldn't grasp how I'd changed, that it was forgetting he could as well. But I was ready for this.

"Dax, shift back to human form," I told him none-too-gently.

He growled—a deep throated, hair rising sound that made my fight or flight instincts thrum. It also pissed me off to no end. No matter how many times I'd been growled at like that by troubled werewolves, it always had the same effect. Maybe it was because I was trying so hard to help them, maybe it was because my will to live was so strong. Whatever the reason, it enraged me to the point where fear and caution burned from my system faster than setting fire to Spirytus Vodka.

Lips pulled back from gnashing teeth, Dax crouched, muscles bunching as he prepared to launch himself at me.

"Shift!" I screamed at Dax, pouring all that fury into the word, making it a command.

A whimper and spittle shot from his lips. He flinched backwards, hunched down, and tucked his tail between his legs. Before it could fully curl beneath him, his body vibrated, blurred, and shifted back to human form. Wide eyes gazed up at me from where he crouched on all fours in the snow. A heartbeat later those eyes rolled up into his head, his lids drooped closed, and he collapsed face first into the snow.

Sighing, I shook my head as I approached him. "Sorry, kid. I didn't want it to go this way, but you gave me no choice."

Sighing, I scooped Dax up and carried him into the cave. Thankfully, I only had a few dozen feet to go, which was why I'd let him chase me back here. After a long night of running, the less distance I had to carry him, the better, werewolf strength or not. I tucked him into his sleeping bag, threw on a long jacket, and set to building a fire.

If tomorrow didn't go better, this kid was doomed. While it would be horrible any time, the last thing I wanted was to lose a troubled to madness so close to the holiday. But if he didn't get control of his instincts, of his wolf, by the night after tomorrow, there would be nothing more I could do for him. To succumb to madness meant a death sentence.

4

"I'm so, so sorry," Dax said for at least the fifth time since waking up.

Out of placating comments, I finished the last bite of my lunch instead of answering. It was past two in the afternoon and he had only been awake for a little over an hour. Being forced by another to shift like I'd done to him took a lot out of a person. That was the least of the reasons I hated to do it, though.

Setting my plate aside, I leaned closer to the fire and responded. "Hang onto that guilt, remember it when you are in wolf form tonight. Let it ground you and remind you of your human side. Remembering you're human will help you control your wolf's instincts."

He swallowed hard, gaze fixating on the flickering flames between us. "If I can't control my wolf tonight, will *she* be here tomorrow?"

"No," I told him. "The day after." No sense in prettying up the hard truth. If he took longer than tonight and tomorrow, he would lose himself completely to the instincts of his wolf and go mad. If that happened, he would have to be put down because he'd become an indiscriminate killer. Allowing an insane werewolf to live put all of our kind in danger of exposure.

"Will it be quick?" he whispered.

I threw a can of beer at him, startling him and making him focus on me. He caught it on instinct.

"You won't have to worry about that because you're going to get control of this," I said with complete confidence.

The feel of his power told me he had the potential to get a handle on this, but the stench of his fear meant he might not.

"You really think so?" he asked.

"I know so."

He let out a long breath and popped open his beer.

We spent the next hour or so putting back a few cold ones and chatting about the plus side of being a *varúlfur*. The conversation involved a lot of joking and laughing by design. I even got him to eat something. The golden hour before sunset snuck up on us. The moon made its way onto the horizon, pulling Dax upright like a puppet on strings.

"Remember what we talked about. Think about the reason for the instinct and it will help keep your human side focused and present," I said as I stood.

His breathing grew shallow.

"It's all good. Let's not ruin your clothes today, huh?" I said through a crooked grin.

Though he smiled in return, his lips pulled a little too tight. Thankfully, he took his borrowed T-shirt off and reached for the waistband of his sweatpants—which I'd been pleased to find at the cave when we returned, no doubt courtesy of my amazing boyfriend. I turned to the side and started to strip.

"Let the shift happen, natural and easy," I said. "And if you get panicked, remember that Yule celebration happening next week in Hemlock Hollow. You don't want to miss it."

Though I didn't turn to look, I heard him suck in a deep breath and blow it out slowly, and knew he was getting ready. "Do you want to see me shift first?" I asked.

A sharper intake of breath along with the sudden stench of sweat made me turn his way. All the blood had drained from his face and he shook with the effort of fighting the change.

"The wolf is part of you and you are part of it. Relax and become one with it," I said in my most soothing tone.

He began gasping, clearly only moments from a full-on panic attack. Before I could even worry about keeping my gaze above his waist, he shook violently, then flowed into wolf form. Once again, he took off like a shot. Cursing, I shifted and hit all fours running. It was going to be another long night.

This night ended much the same as the prior. Part of me knew I should be glad he gave in to the instinct of flight instead of fight, but the rest of me was too worried to be glad about any of it. Being the actual night of the full moon, it was the hardest one for him. I expected that. But in the end, I'd hoped he'd be able to shift back on his own. And again, I'd had to force him. The next day he slept even longer than the first. While he did, I texted Ty and Ayra, letting them know I was okay and that Dax was doing good. Too bad he wasn't. The worst part was, as the reaper of shifterkind, Ayra would know I was lying. She no doubt felt the pull of Dax's nearly mad power. If he tipped over from troubled to condemned, she would be here in a heartbeat.

Throughout the morning we watched snow fall outside the cave, muffling all sounds and smells. After lunch and a chat about his sad past as a reclusive call center guy with no friends or future, an idea formed. Among other things, I told him all about how Hemlock Hollow went crazy for the holiday, decorating the entire town, along with a living seventy-foot-tall Canadian hemlock in the park in the middle of town. Dax relaxed, all traces of fear melting away more with each minute that passed.

"It sounds nice, better than any holiday I've ever had," he said in a soft voice, picking at ice built up on a rock.

"Yeah, it is pretty great. There are three packs in town, and they are always looking to add more members to their family," I said, making it sound like something that didn't make my skin crawl. A team player I was not.

His wide-eyed gaze locked on me. "Really?" Then his face fell. "Yeah, but what would they want with a guy like me? I'm just a tech nerd, not a fighter."

"So, there's this guy called Einstein—"

"No shit, Sherlock," he interrupted.

I smiled. "That's just what they call him. His real name is Einar. Anyway, Einstein designs all kinds of cool gadgets like satellite blockers that blanket the town in a kind of black out space so the packs can't be spied on."

"Seriously? That's government level stuff," he said.

Like the scout I'd never been, I raised two fingers. "I swear." It was true, so it wasn't hard to sound convincing. "And that's only one of the cool things he has designed. What I'm getting at is you don't have to be a fighter to be valuable to the packs. You could find a place among them, a family, a purpose."

Hope filled his eyes as he swallowed hard. "You really think so?"

"I know it," I said with complete confidence, because I would make sure of it. One way or another, this young man would find a place to belong.

The purest joy I'd ever seen spread across his face in the wake of a huge smile. With it, a light seemed to go in inside him, making his power all but glow. I stood and began to undress.

"But it's not time," he protested.

I set my shoes inside the cave. "The moon sways us, but it doesn't rule us. Shift now and we avoid the pressure," I said nice and casual, like it was no big deal.

After putting the last of my clothing in my duffle bag, I walked barefoot out into the snow. When I didn't hear him following, I called back in a teasing tone. "You're not going to make me stand out here naked in the snow, are you?"

I heard the soft sound of clothes landing on a rock in the cave, followed by footsteps. Reaching for the ground, I shifted to my wolf form. After a good shake of my black fur, I turned to look back at Dax. He swallowed hard as he stared wide-eyed at me. I wagged my tail. A small laugh slipped from him. I grinned, tongue lolling out the side of my mouth to keep the expression unaggressive.

He shifted, landing on all fours so abruptly his canine nose buried in the snow. Laughter chuffed from me. Sniffing, he narrowed clear eyes at me—eyes in which I saw both his human and wolf sides. Hope bubbled up in me like the head of a properly poured beer. I beckoned with my snout in a very human gesture for him to follow me. Together we jogged across the snowy landscape toward the forest.

Everything went nice and smooth, until the shadows of twilight began to stretch across the land and the moon rose in a navy sky painted purple along the horizon. Unfortunately, we'd just caught the scent of a rabbit. Normally that wouldn't be unfortunate. If one didn't count the indigestion I always got the day after eating a raw meal in wolf form. But with Dax being so new at this, it spiked his aggression level into the stratosphere.

Lips curled back from his fangs through which a vicious snarl emerged, he stepped between me and the rabbit. Large, fluffy looking flakes of snow began to fall. It failed to soften the moment. His shifter power snapped and popped like a pitchy Yule log. I shook my head in another intentionally human gesture. He needed to think, and I hoped me acting out of character for a wolf would help. Ears pricking up, his head cocked to the side.

Suddenly, the rabbit bolted out from the brush—straight toward me. I stumbled back, almost stepping on it in my haste. Dax let out a savage growl and leaped for me. At the last moment, I dodged and swiped out at him with a paw. Wicked fast, he snapped at me, grazing one of the pads of my foot. Pain shot through it.

This time when Dax came at me I placed my front paws on his chest, rolled to my back, put my rear feet on his stomach, and threw him judo roll style. He went flying. A surprised whimper and rush of air escaped him as he landed in a heap.

In a heartbeat I was on him—literally. I pinned him with my front paws on his chest and my jaws around his throat. He went utterly still. To press the point home, I gave his throat a little shake, careful not to let my fangs break the skin. When I let go and stepped away, he remained on the ground. Only his tail moved, slowly working its way up to curl against his stomach.

I huffed and lifted my paw to evaluate the wound. A deep slice cut across the length of the palm pad. The dull throbbing that started when I put weight on it made me growl. Dax whined. After giving him a long, hard look, I gestured with my head for him to follow. Not looking back to see if he did—because I had to keep up the whole alpha act—I trotted off. What he did in the next few hours would determine whether he lived to see another moonrise.

5

The scents of blood and snow mingled in the frosty air. Each step I took left a crimson paw print, startlingly bright against the pure white. The cut on my right hand—paw, since I was in wolf form—burned like a mother. Doing my best to ignore it, I loped across the valley nestled between two tall mountain peaks so white they looked more like glaciers. Or, at least, what I thought glaciers would look like. I couldn't really say since I hadn't seen one yet. Stars peaked through the cloudy night sky here and there. The brush with violence seemed to be making me appreciate the landscape anew.

The wonderful scent of fire led me to the cave mouth. Embers snapped and popped as flames licked at the logs of fir piled into the fire pit. I hadn't left a fire going, which meant someone had been here. It didn't surprise me, considering that if I was going to need help with Dax, it would be tonight. The only question was, who—Ty or Ayra?

I gave one good shake of my black fur, starting at my muzzle and ending at the tip of my bushy tail. Snow flew from me in every direction. Bracing myself, I triggered the shift with a thought.

"Ugh," I grunted as I rose from my hands and knees.

With each step toward the cave, I sank at least a solid foot into the soft, fresh powder. Snow and ice clung in places a person should never have snow and ice—an unfortunate side effect of getting it all over one's fur, then shifting. Despite my naturally higher body temperature, I shivered. Once inside, the knee-deep snow gave way to the freezing, rocky cave floor. Wincing at how my bare feet stuck a bit, I sped toward the flickering fire. At least it was better than sinking into the snow.

I grabbed one of the fluffy robes from where they lay folded on a boulder and put it on. The robes were new as well, and very much appreciated. Sitting, I propped my feet onto one of the rocks surrounding the roaring fire. Orange and yellow flames danced inches away from my toes. A long sigh eased from my lungs as searing warmth seeped into me. It kickstarted my werewolf metabolism, which heated me up from within until the sub-zero temperature of the cave felt like a balmy sixty degrees or more. Looking down at the gash across my palm, I winced. Why did wounds always hurt more once a person saw the blood?

Soft lupine footsteps padded outside the cave. It was a subtle sound—the compacting of snow beneath four padded paws, but unmistakable. The gait was clumsy, almost like Dax tripped every other step. Outside the cave, snow had begun to fall lightly, making it hard to see much further than thirty feet or so beyond the entrance. From out of the white haze slinked Dax's huge grey wolf form. He stopped at the edge of the entrance and gave a querulous whine.

I beckoned to the fire. "Come in. Get out of the storm," I invited.

Blood dripped from my hand, sizzling as it hit the wood in the fire. The wolf's yellow eyes widened, and it lowered its head, hesitating.

"Don't sweat it. I've had worse. I'll heal. In the end, you gained control and that's what matters," I said.

Staying low to the ground in a cross between a crouch and a crawl, he entered the cave and slinked to the fire. The scent of wet canine assaulted my nose. I grabbed the other robe and held it out.

"Shift back. It will be your final test," I instructed, doing my best to make it a statement instead of a command.

This time I needed him to do it. If it wasn't of his own free will, all of this would mean nothing.

Golden eyes blinking closed, his furry nose scrunched up. Heat radiated from him, but nothing happened. He began to pant. The furrows along the top of his snout deepened.

"You have to want it. Overcome the instinct with rational thought. Think about why you want to be human," I instructed. That he even listened was a good sign. I hoped.

His panting stopped. The creases along his snout and between his closed eyes smoothed out. His entire body shimmered and flowed. A heartbeat later, he crouched on the cave floor in human form.

"Well done," I said as I threw the robe at him. He put it on and settled onto a rock on the opposite side of the fire from me.

He gave me the most awkward bow I'd ever seen anyone attempt and tilted his head to the side, baring his neck. "Thank you, exalted Seeker. Does this mean I'm not going to go crazy?" he asked.

Smacking a hand over my eyes, I cringed. They acted this way sometimes, like I'd performed some sort of miracle when in reality it was them and their own will power. "Don't call me that, and definitely not like that. You're safe, you beat it."

A long, very loud sigh whooshed from him. "So no date with the—what was the word you used for her, *uppskera*?"

He butchered the Hemlock Hollow dialect of the Icelandic term for "reaper," but considering how scared and hopeful he sounded, I wasn't going to call him out on it.

"Not for you," I confirmed.

Tears spilled from his eyes. I grinned behind my hair, soaking up the warmth.

Silent as only a truly talented apex predator can be, a tall blond man stepped out of the dark into the glow cast by the fire. "You better wipe those tears off. They will freeze to your cheeks in this weather." He tossed a bundle of clothes to Dax, followed by a pair of shoes he dropped on the ground next to him.

The sound of his voice vibrated along my skin and power in a delicious way that made me want to rub against him. He gave me a heart-stopping smile and shook snow from his jacket.

The young man flinched, grabbed the clothes, and scurried deeper into the cave away from Ty.

"Ty," I said, in a bit of a breathy voice. I couldn't help it. The man had that effect on me. "We've got it under control, but thanks for bringing the clothes."

One blond brow rose as his gaze went from a bloody spot in the snow, then to me. "Hmmm," he grunted, clearly not quite agreeing.

Removing a small pouch from his brown jacket, he knelt down beside me. He unzipped the pouch and took out a bottle of hydrogen peroxide. With a pointed look, he held out his hand.

"That's not necessary. It'll be healed in a few days," I said.

Head cocked to the side, his gaze flicked to the newly bitten werewolf hiding in the back of the cave. "Yes, but who knows what kind of infection you may get from his claws."

Groaning and rolling my eyes, I offered up my palm to make him happy. The liquid stung as it hit the wound, then promptly fizzed up as if to prove Ty right. Warmth and pleasure caused by his touch eclipsed the pain. As he dabbed at it with a bit of gauze, he sniffed the air around me. "Is that the only wound?"

"It is. He only lost control for a moment," I said.

He grunted his disapproval.

From the back of the cave came a slight whine from Dax. "I didn't mean to hurt her. The instinct to fight, to kill, was so strong at first. But I'm good now, I promise. Right, Seeker?"

I narrowed my eyes at Ty, hoping the glare communicated my disapproval of his harshness toward the newly bitten. "Yes, Dax, you're good. It's all downhill from here. And don't worry, Ty isn't the reaper."

A very loud, very relieved sigh came from him. He knew it was a woman, but in his state of fear, he clearly doubted that knowledge.

"Nope, I am the protective boyfriend," Ty said.

Growling, I smacked Ty's rock-hard arm. "Go easy on the kid. He's had a rough three days, and this is going

34

to be his first holiday as a werewolf, and he has no family to spend it with."

The look on Ty's face softened, and guilt filled his glacial blue eyes. "I know, and I do feel bad for him. I got a hold of the Hemlock Hollow Alpha Council, and they have assigned him a *kennari* already. He will spend the holiday with them."

A *kennari*—or teacher—was typically only assigned once the newly bitten made it through the becoming successfully. While Dax was over the hard part, he still had a lot to learn.

I sat up and cupped Ty's left cheek. "Ah, Ty, thank you. That was so sweet." He almost never contacted the Council prior to me getting the newly bitten through their third night, the one after the full moon. Close to a third of newly bitten weren't able to overcome instinct and control their wolf. Which was why the council liked to wait.

Once Ty finished cleaning the wound, I kissed him lightly on the lips. "You're the best. And thanks for the fire, that was nice to come back to, but I'm eager to get home to our bed."

"Of course. Dax can stay in the guest room for tonight since it's so late. I will take him to his *kennari* tomorrow."

"Perfect," I said as I pulled my jeans on. "I can get a good night's sleep before my big day tomorrow with Ayra."

"Big day?" Dax asked.

My lips split into a huge smile. "Holiday shopping." It wasn't like me to get excited about holiday shopping, but then, I'd never had a reason, what with no friends and my family putting the strange in estranged. But this year was different.

Eyes popping wide open, Dax gaped at me. "It's two days before Christmas! Boy, you like to live on the edge."

I snickered. He had no idea how accurate his observation was. My shopping partner, and best friend second only to Ty, was none other than the reaper herself.

6

I slipped up Ayra's white, winding, freshly plowed driveway lined with four-foot-tall candy canes. Timing it just right, I eased the Jeep to a stop before her two-story log cabin. Double tiered planting beds framed a stone walkway that led up to the huge covered deck. Of course nothing was in them now but snow. The snow up here in Hemlock Hollow was even deeper than back home outside of Missoula, three feet easily. Sure, I could have put the Jeep in four-wheel drive and not slid at all, but where was the fun in that?

Strings of multicolored lights lined every peak and edge of the house, framed every window and door, including the walkway. At night they probably made this place glow and put a strain on the solar panels lining the metal roof. It made me smile to think Ayra, the reaper of shifterkind, lived in one of the most festive houses I'd ever seen.

Grateful for whoever had shoveled the walkway, I grabbed my canvas bag of presents, jumped out onto the icy flagstones, and started for the house. Small snowflakes fell from the sky, landing all over my black hair like dandruff. So much for using the flat iron to smooth it. Here came the frizzies. But I didn't care. I could throw on a cute beanie and call it good. Nothing would dampen my mood today.

The planting beds flanking the stairs looked like beds of marshmallows, all covered in fluffy white snow. It made me want hot chocolate with lots of marshmallows. Maybe I should have had breakfast before coming. In a few more steps the shadow of the covered deck engulfed me, offering a reprieve from the ceaseless snow.

Wooden carvings of bears, one dragging a Yule tree, and the other holding a wreath, sat on either side of the double wooden doors—on each of which hung a fragrant fir wreath decorated with lights, red berries, pinecones, and holly. Next to them sat boots filled with tiny, brightly wrapped presents. I did a double take. Yep, boots. Fist lifted to knock, I stood a moment and stared in awe. Maybe I had gotten the wrong house after all. It wasn't like I'd seen many of the other houses in this town. Several of them could look the same. Montana people were fond of their log cabins and the snow disguised a lot. Before I could think about walking back to the Jeep to check for a house number, the door opened.

The reaper of all shifterkind stood waiting there. A big, orange tabby slinked around Ayra's legs. The cat looked at me, ears rotating, then it turned and sashayed back inside.

"Heimdahlr, you will be civil," Ayra told the cat.

The only indication it heard was another flick of its tail.

In a pair of gray and white camo cargo pants and a white T-shirt with the face of what looked like a red bear on it and the name 'The Rumjacks' above it, Ayra looked fierce. My brows rose.

"You do know we're going shopping, not on a recon trip?" I asked.

Waving a hand, she stepped aside to let me in. "Same thing."

I thought about disagreeing, then realized how close to the holiday we were and knew I had no ground to stand on.

As I stepped inside, my gaze caught on one of the biggest Yule tree I'd seen so far this season—at least fifteen feet tall. It stood next to the staircase and reached almost up to the second story balcony railing. By no means was it the typical perfectly shaped tree one expected, but somehow that made it more beautiful. Multi-colored lights decorated it from top to bottom, along with all manner of ornaments made from natural materials. Next to it, actual fir boughs decorated the railing of the stairway.

I meandered after Ayra, ogling their casually yet perfectly decorated house. Who would have thought my stoic reaper best friend's house would look so festive? Not this girl. She continually shocked me in the most amazing ways, though.

"Your tree looks amazing," I said.

"We take our Yule tree very seriously. The burning of it after the holiday honors Thor as well as invites the return of the sun," she said as she knelt and dug amidst the brightly wrapped presents beneath the tree.

"And the boots outside the door filled with presents? Are those a Yule tradition?" I asked.

She nodded and made a humming noise of affirmation. "They are for the thirteen Yule lads, to keep them from causing mischief."

When she turned around with a burlap wrapped package adorned with a cloth red ribbon in her hand, my expression must have looked as confused as I felt because she burst out laughing—a rare and beautiful gift in itself. "Legend says each day before Yule, one of the lads—trolls really—comes down from the mountains and causes mischief, each a different kind. On the last night their mother, the giantess Grýla, rounds them up and eats them."

Mouth gaping as I tried to process this unique tradition and tale, I just stared at her.

"You think that's weird? You must not have heard about Jólakötturinn," she said.

"Um…no?" I turned the last word into a question, one I wasn't sure I wanted the answer to.

Sitting down on a barstool, she leaned forward with bright eyes. "He's the Yule cat who comes and eats anyone who didn't receive an article of clothing for the holiday."

Legs suddenly feeling weak, I sat my bag on the bar and took a seat next to her. She shook her head. "Ty has been seriously remiss in educating you on our culture. I'm gonna have to talk to him about that."

I chewed on my bottom lip. "Yeah, well, that's probably because his parents are coming from Iceland and I may or may not be freaking out about meeting them for the first time."

Her pale blond brows rose. "That calls for drinks after shopping."

"Definitely," I agreed.

Knowing just when I needed a distraction most, she put a hand on the burlap package with a red ribbon. "I got you a little something too. I hope you're okay with opening it early. I'm not big on the whole opening presents in front of others thing," she said.

Rubbing my hands together, I grinned as I pulled the package into my lap. "Heck yeah. I'm all about early presents! I hope you are too, 'cause I brought yours."

"Sure, but you go first," she pressed.

I didn't have to be told twice. Presents weren't something I'd had a lot of since my dad died. My mother and I hadn't exactly felt festive, so the holidays had all but faded away for us. I tore into the package with a vengeance. One pale brow of Ayra's lifted, but she otherwise remained expressionless. I got the distinct feeling my enthusiasm amused her. Inside the package lay something knitted from a beautiful forest green yarn, cinched together in the middle with a gorgeous silver cuff covered in knotwork that formed a tree.

Gasping, I took it out. The yarn felt like butter against my skin. The cuff slid from it with a soft "whisp". The yarn turned out to be a long, gorgeous scarf. I wrapped it around my neck and rubbed my cheek against it. The thing had to have cost a fortune. And the cuff...I couldn't stop staring at it.

"These are beautiful, Ayra. This scarf feels like alpaca yarn. It must have cost a fortune, and this bracelet...I just... Wow."

She waved a hand. "It *is* alpaca, but I crocheted it myself, so it didn't cost nearly what you think."

A lump formed in my throat at the words. Tears blurred my vision as I looked up at her. "You *made* this?" I whispered.

With a shrug, she nodded like it was no big deal. My reaper best friend, slayer of shifters who went insane and turned into killing monsters, had crocheted me a scarf. A tear escaped my left eye and left a hot trail down my cheek.

Alarm widened her eyes. "Oh no, what's wrong? You aren't allergic to alpaca wool are you? Is it hideous? You don't have to pretend it isn't," she said, reaching for it like she might take it away.

I clutched it against me. "No, I'm not allergic and it isn't hideous. It is the most beautiful thing anyone has ever given me. It's just, it's been a long time since anyone made something especially for me."

She smiled. "Well, we couldn't have Jólakötturinn coming to eat you."

My eyes widened before returning to the cuff. "And this, it's..." I searched my memories of dad's stories for the name.

"Yggdrasil, the world tree, the center of the cosmos, the thing that holds it all together with its branches and roots. Like you and the way you hold all of us together, me, Vidar, and Ty," she said.

After slipping the cuff around my wrist I stood and pulled her into an embrace. Stiff as a stone statue, she stood there and endured it. But beneath the hard shell, I felt the warmth of her power and I knew she welcomed the affection. I let go and all but skipped back to the canvas bag I'd placed on the bar. I pulled the small package wrapped in green and white from it and handed it to her.

"Now you!"

One corner of her mouth rose in the semblance of a smile that made *me* smile all the wider. She took the package in her hands like it was a fragile thing that might break. Extending a claw, she proceeded to meticulously cut the tape on the sides and bottom and unwrapped it ever so slowly. I chewed my lip and bounced a knee.

"How can you be so calm? The suspense is killing me!" I exclaimed.

From behind her white-blond hair I caught her smile growing.

"Oh, oh you're messing with me," I said.

Without looking up, she countered in a deadpan tone, "I am not. This is simply how I open presents."

As she opened the tiny box, she sat up a little straighter. She went so quiet and still it ratcheted my anxiety up a dozen notches. Her hand shook as she drew the silver pendant out. I must have screwed it up.

"Oh no, did I get it wrong? It's supposed to be a bind rune of Gebo from Freyr's Aett for friendship and harmony, and the Berkana from Tyr's Aett for new beginnings and family, our family, the four of us," I said, starting to feel like I was rambling. The way she stared down at it, mouth hanging open, made me think I'd made some terrible cultural faux paus. Maybe I would get eaten by the Yule cat after all.

When she finally looked up, her eyes shone with moisture. "You got it exactly right. It's beautiful and perfect," she whispered, voice sounding choked.

I blew out a breath. "That's a relief! I was going to have to give Ty a piece of my mind if I had gotten it wrong because he helped me make it. We actually created the mold out of this black sand stuff, melted down the silver and poured it ourselves. Did you know he had a mini forge? He really rocks the Viking look all sweaty and working over a forge." More rambling, but this time it was happy rambling—and a touch uncomfortable rambling at making the reaper tear up.

When we'd made the pendant, I'd felt the thrum of power coursing from me into it.

She put it on, the chain making it hang just high enough above her valknut necklace—three intermingled triangles honoring the fallen dead, and showing fealty to Odin. The two looked good together, right. Fingers lingering on it, she looked down and I pretended not to notice it was because she was hiding her tear-filled eyes from me.

Rubbing her hands together, she looked up with a smile that sent a chill through me. "All right, let's go shopping!"

"Only a sadist enjoys shopping the week of the holiday," I said.

Head cocked, she did a one shoulder shrug before sliding from the bar stool.

As we walked toward the door, a thought occurred to me. "I hope the necklace counts as a piece of clothing, because I can't crochet to save my life."

7

An extra spring in my step helped me pull my boots out of the three feet of snow piled beside the storefront I'd inadvertently walked into. With my treasures tucked securely in the reusable canvas shopping bag slung over my shoulder, I finally felt ready for the big day—which lay only two days away. Never in my life had I had so many people to shop for—Ty, Ayra, Vidar, and Candice, I'd even grabbed a little something for Dax. And I loved it. Making friends had never been my thing. Between taking care of my mother and going through med school, there hadn't been time.

The bell on the shop door chimed, followed immediately by laughter as Ayra stepped out after me. Unlike me, she didn't get distracted by the pretty holiday display in the store window and wander into a snowbank. The sound of her laughter was such a rare thing that it took a second to get over my shock and join in. I'd heard it more today than in the entire time I'd known her. The sight of her extremely slight frame—that deceptively hid a lot of hardened muscle—doubled over as she held her stomach, and long, white-blond braid nearly touching the icy sidewalk, soon had me laughing so hard tears sprung to my eyes.

We recovered eventually and started down the slick sidewalk to where I'd parked the Jeep half a block away. "Hey, this *varúlfur* thing should come with a natural grace or something. I feel like I got robbed in that department," I joked. In the mixed company of normal humans, as we were here in Missoula, I had to use the Icelandic term for werewolf if I didn't want to sound crazy—which I most definitely did not.

She let out one more small laugh. "Yeah, no such luck there."

Nose to the grey sky, I made a sniffling noise. "What good are superpowers if you can't look cool?"

Ever so carefully—as if afraid I might topple on the ice, which I might—she bumped me with her elbow. "Looking cool is overrated," she said.

I elbow-bumped her back. "Agreed."

We had almost reached the Jeep when she threw a massive wrench in my entire holiday. "So what did you get Ty for *Jólabókaflóðið*?"

Keys in hand, I pulled up short just before stepping off the curb. "For what? Can you say that again, slower?"

She did. It didn't help.

"What is that, exactly?" I sincerely hoped she was making it up to mess with me. She had a weird, cop-like sense of dry humor, so it wouldn't surprise me.

Hefting her own canvas shopping bags into the Jeep, she gave me a deadpan look. I wasn't swayed. It could still be a joke.

"It's an Icelandic holiday tradition to buy your loved ones a book and give it to them on Solstice Eve. Everyone sits around and reads their new books, eating cookies and drinking *jólabland*," she insisted.

Frowning at her, I climbed in and shut my door. "Are you messing with me?"

She held her fuzzy-blue-gloved hands up. "Not in the least."

"Swear to Odin?" I pressed, knowing she wouldn't take such an oath lightly.

"Swear to Odin."

I started the Jeep, which complained a bit about the cold before finally turning over. "Okay, I'll bite. What's *jólabland*?"

"The Hemlock Hollow version is half your favorite stout beer and half orange soda." I must have made a face because she held her hands up. "Hey, don't knock it before you try it. It's actually pretty good."

Though I still wasn't entirely convinced, I wasn't about to rain on her parade either. Ayra had been through a lot in her life, and this holiday season was the first one she might have ever gotten the chance to enjoy. No brother beating her up, no parents berating her for every wrongly perceived, little flaw. For that matter, it was the first I'd been able to enjoy in a long time too. I had friends to share it with, not to mention an incredible boyfriend that may have literally hung the moon—in my not-so-humble opinion.

"In that case, I guess we're not done shopping. So where are some good bookstores in Missoula?"

With a grin, she pulled out her phone and brought up a mapping app. I'd never seen her smile this much, and it warmed me more than my half-broke heater stuck on high ever could. I cranked up the holiday music and started singing as I pulled out onto the treacherously white road. She gave me serious side-eye, but I noticed the corner of her lip twitching in an attempt not to smile.

An hour and three bookstores later, my holiday cheer began to wear dangerously thin. I all but growled at the tall cowboy who tipped his hat as he held open the door for us to enter.

"Sorry, she's over-caffeinated," Ayra apologized for me as she walked past.

Great, I was so testy the reaper of all shifter kind was apologizing on my behalf. A self-depreciating groan slipped from me as I laid eyes on the cozy store.

Row upon row of standing shelves packed the small space. Classic holiday music poured cheerily through speakers mounted in the corners of the room. Lights hung from the ceiling in random clusters that managed a cool, fairy-lights look. Books towered in precarious piles at the end of several rows, looking like they may topple with the slightest touch. A little, fake holiday tree packed with superhero ornaments and glowing with white lights crowded into one aisle. Brightly colored, illustrated covers popped out at me from every shelf—comic books and graphic novels. To our left stretched a long counter behind which stood a young man with his nose buried in a Manga novel. He didn't so much as look up at us.

Lifting a brow, I turned to Ayra. "A comic bookstore? You brought me to a comic bookstore?"

"Yep." Though her voice remained deadpan as always, I noticed a twinkle in her eye and a spring in her step as she strode into the store.

It made me remember something she'd once told me. "That's right, you and Vidar love comic books," I said with a smile.

"Since we were kids," she said, just a touch of wistfulness in her tone.

She'd told me of how she and Vidar used to lay in the meadow and read comic books until the daylight faded. "Then we're bound to find the perfect *Jolabolkaflodid* gift for him here!" I exclaimed.

"*Jólabókaflóðið,*" she said.

"Yeah, that's what I said."

Her pale brows rose into her equally pale blond hair. "That is most definitely *not* what you said."

I grimaced. "It's not?"

"No."

Shoulders rising, I shook my head. "Sue me. My Icelandic is far from perfect."

She grinned at that. "It's not so bad."

The slightly musty but oh-so-wonderful scent of old books wafted around us as we walked deeper into the store. "And you're a terrible liar, but it's nice of you to support my fluency delusions."

"That's what friends are for," she said. "It roughly translates to 'Christmas book flood'."

"Doesn't have the same ring to it," I said.

"I know, right?"

As she picked up a comic book, I made my way around to the other side of the low shelf.

"You and Vidar are coming over for this thing, right?" I asked.

"No." The complete lack of inflection in her voice made me rise up onto my toes to get a peek at her expression. Stoic as ever, she gave nothing away.

"But you're our best friends. You have to. The holidays are all about friends," I pressed.

A look I'd never seen on her face before lit up her features—wonder. "You really want to spend the holiday with us?" The guarded tone of her voice made my heart hurt for her a little. But the way one hand strayed to the necklace I got her eased the pain.

"Of course. You guys are our pack—well, as much of one as we'll ever claim."

One pale brow went up. "You are an odd seeker, Sonya Michaelson."

"So you guys will come?"

"No."

I let out an exasperated breath. "Why not?"

She looked at me full-on with her reaper stare. "Because you're meeting Ty's parents for the first time. Having us there will only make it...awkward."

"I don't care. You have to come. I won't take no for an answer."

"Fine, but not for *Jólabókaflóðið*. We'll come the day after for Solstice dinner."

I smiled. "Deal."

Browsing, I wandered, hoping something would catch my eye. "What kind of book does one buy a history professor?" I wondered, mostly to myself.

After a moment, Ayra spoke. "Maybe you're thinking of it wrong."

"How so?"

"Don't think of what he does for a living. Think of who he is, what he enjoys outside of work," Ayra said.

I wanted to smack myself on the forehead. It seemed so obvious, and yet, I hadn't shopped for anyone in a very, very long time. Holidays had never been my thing. My mother was usually in rehab—as she was now—or missing in action, I had no real friends over the years, and I tended to stay single around the holidays. But Ty, Ayra, and Vidar had changed all of that.

While my gaze scanned the shelves, I thought about what Ayra had said. Blue and silver hues snagged my attention. A cover made me smile. It was an illustration in shades of black, red, and grey of a couple from the hips down. With blood dripping from the title, it reminded me of the vampire movies Ty and I loved to watch together.

"That's perfect," I whispered as I picked it up.

Ayra appeared over my shoulder as if she had materialized there. If I didn't spend every day surrounded by werewolves, it might have made me jump. The fact that she was the most dangerous one alive probably should have made me leap like an Olympian. But I'd never been good at doing what I was supposed to. She hummed as she leaned closer. "*Bitten by Surprise*, that looks steamy and interesting," she said.

"It does, doesn't it?" I turned it over to read the back. It had me at "psychic" and "vampire".

"Oh hey, that's by Lizzy Gayle. I love her books!" Ayra said with uncharacteristic enthusiasm. She grabbed another copy off the shelf and tucked it against her chest into a growing stack of at least three others. The reaper of shifterkind loved to read. Who knew?

"How am I just now finding out you love to read more than comic books? Not that comic books aren't reading, because they definitely are. And you have outstanding taste in books, by the way, if the reviews of this book are any indication," I asked.

She gave a non-committal half-shrug. "I have layers."

That may be the understatement of the century. I laughed. "Yes, my sister, you do," I said as I eyed the comic books on the bottom of her stack. Letting out a deep sigh, I turned back to the shelves. "Now, what to get Ty's parents?"

Ayra shrugged. "You're on your own for that one."

We perused the cramped store through another three holiday songs before ending up at a table affectionately labeled "Mystery Gifts". Books of all shapes and sizes wrapped in cheery red and green paper sat stacked beneath genre tags. What the hell. I was out of ideas. "Hmm, I think Ty mentioned his mom liking Irish folklore fantasy," I said as I picked up one with a sparkly jute ribbon.

Face completely stoic, Ayra raised one brow at me. "Living on the edge, hm?" she asked in her signature monotone that everyone else mistook for being emotionless but I knew was the opposite.

Laughing, I bumped her shoulder with mine. "Yep, that's me."

Her brow rose higher until it disappeared beneath her furry white hat. She blinked slowly at me. Without a word, she handed me a book.

"What's this?" I asked.

"For Ty's father."

"Thought I was on my own?"

She shrugged.

The cover portrayed a smiling man in a suit. It was an autobiography by a congressman. "He likes non-fiction?" I asked, tone doubtful. Just saying non-fiction put a bad taste in my mouth.

"He'll like this. The man is…" she leaned in close and whispered, "*varúlfur*."

My world exploded a little more like it always did when another secret of the hidden supernatural world revealed itself to me. Apparently, our kind held high places in politics. That was news to me. "Oh. That'll do."

"Good, because if I have to listen to another song about jingly bells, Odin so help me, we will call lightning down on this place," Ayra said.

Her serious tone made me bust up laughing so hard it soon doubled me over.

Though her face remained utterly humorless, the sparkle in her eyes warmed my heart. The fact that she'd had a good time today made it worth it, even if Ty and his parents hated everything I bought them.

8

The natural bristles of the bamboo toothbrush splayed out in a fan pattern from the rigorous way I worked at the grout of the kitchen counter. It looked clean, but I could almost swear I smelled something. What if it was missed fluids from that time Ty had taken me right here?

Oh Gods, his parents might smell that! I scrubbed harder.

A knock sounded on the door, making me jump half out of my skin, literally. Fangs and claws sprang in an instinctual response to getting surprised so suddenly. I forced them to retract and kept scrubbing.

"Sonya? I can hear you cleaning. I know you are not going to the bathroom. You are cleaning again," Ty's voice came through the closed door.

"I smell something. It might be sex."

"No, that would be cleaner with a hint of lemon. The entire cabin smells like it now."

"No, I think it's sex."

A little pop sounded behind me and the door opened. I turned to see Ty's impressive six-foot-five inches leaning against the doorframe, corded arms crossed beneath pectorals as hard as granite. One blond eyebrow was quirked. "It is most definitely not sex. If you would like, I would be happy to remind you exactly how that smells."

I flushed as my blood heated and rushed straight to my groin where muscles I hadn't used in a week clenched. We'd been so busy with the holiday preparations we hadn't found the time to do much more than cuddle. Okay, that wasn't entirely true. I was terrified that if we had sex in the house, his parents would smell it. And there was six feet of snow outside, so...

Capturing me with his glacial blue eyes that somehow managed to burn with an unquenchable fire, he advanced on me. Before I knew it, his body pressed against mine and he pulled the battered toothbrush from my hand.

"I need you," he said with enough feeling to make my knees go weak.

His arms wrapped around me, pulled me tighter against him, then cupped my ass. "Ty, I just spent the last week scrubbing every sign that we ever had sex in this house away. No way in Helheimr are we undoing all that work because you're horny."

One hand massaged my right butt cheek while the other worked its way up my back beneath my shirt. My nipples grew as hard as ball bearings as he neared my bra. Suddenly, he withdrew, using his werewolf speed to ghost over to the doorframe and lean casually against it again. "Well, if you are not horny, I can be patient. Though my parents will be here an entire week."

Groaning, I closed my eyes and let my head fall back against the medicine cabinet. "I most definitely didn't say I wasn't, but the thought of them sitting somewhere we had sex and smelling the evidence..." I groaned again and squeezed my eyes shut tight. Why did werewolves have to have such an incredible sense of smell?

"Mortifies you," he finished for me.

When I opened my eyes and nodded, he stood directly before me once again. He took one of my hands in his. "Sonya, werewolves embrace their instincts. You know this. Sex is one of the strongest instincts we possess. I assure you, my parents know we have sex, and they approve."

Crying out in protest, I covered my face with my free hand. "Nope, can't go there. Can't deal with thinking about that."

He chuckled and pulled my hand away from my face. "While I am not going to lie—I would love to have sex with you right now—that is not what I need you for at the moment," he said.

"Oh. Okay, what then? Are we out of something? Oh no, it's cranberries, isn't it? Dammit, I forgot the cranberries!" Panic started to set in and narrow my vision.

I'd never done the holiday thing with a family. The boyfriends I'd had over the years weren't the kind that took me home to the parents. To make matters worse, this was the first time I was meeting Ty's parents. I wanted this to be perfect for them and especially for him. My disfunction had a high probability of ruining it for everyone, so I had to take every precaution I could.

Expression full of love and tolerance, Ty took my face gently in his hands. "We have plenty of cranberries. I think you bought six pounds."

I smiled. "Well, werewolves eat a lot."

He laughed. "Not even four werewolves can eat that many cranberries in one sitting."

Okay, I might have overdone it a bit, and not just with the shopping. Letting out a little laugh that belied my nervousness, I shrugged. "You said your dad liked them. So what is it you need my help with?"

After placing a maddeningly chaste kiss on my lips, he took my hand and led me through the huge cabin with its mixture of semi-modern furnishings and rustic log work to the living room.

"We are missing one very important thing," he said.

My stomach tightened in a sickening knot. "Oh no, what?"

"I have been so busy grading papers, and you have been so busy with that newly bitten that we have not gotten our Yule tree."

The knot tightened so severely and quickly I thought I might actually throw up. How could I have forgotten such a thing? "Oh no. Oh no." I may have repeated it a few more times. I couldn't be sure because panic fully set in.

"Do not worry, I have a plan. Here," Ty said, grabbing my jacket off the back of the large L-shaped couch dominating the space in front of the real wood-burning fireplace.

He escorted me to the shoe bench in the foyer. As I put my coat on, he grabbed what I referred to as my utilitarian boots from the closet. They were real leather, brown, waterproof, and came to mid-calf—not exactly cute or even attractive in my opinion, but they were great for bad weather. I gave Ty my best one-brow-raised look—which was to say I squinted awkwardly in what probably appeared like I had something in my eye. If we were heading to a tree lot in town, I was not about to wear those. Suspicion tickled at the back of my neck.

"You want me to wear these into town?" I asked.

He gave me a smirk that could melt edible panties. The man's eyes could twinkle like nobody's business, and right now, they were twinkling like a clear night sky in Montana.

61

"No. I want you to wear them into the woods," he said in all seriousness, as if there weren't six feet of snow outside.

That left me utterly speechless, mouth gaping.

Ty's eyes widened and he started to look a bit flustered. "Well, you said you wanted to start our own traditions. I thought a good start might be hunting for our Yule tree on our own property, then replanting one in the spring together."

The vulnerable tone of his voice washed away any reservations I had. And those eyes, so gorgeous and blue, were something I couldn't say no to. Not even if my idea of creating our own traditions had been more along the lines of drinking perfectly mixed eggnog by the fire or watching holiday movies based off Wren Michaels and Poppy Minnix's books.

Before I knew it, I was properly bundled, and Ty whisked me out the door into the brisk morning. A perfect, thick blanket of snow covered everything, weighing down the pine boughs of the trees surrounding the yard. The plowed turnabout in front of the cabin looked as though someone had carved a path through a glacier, leaving walls over seven feet tall to each side. Above it all, the sun shone down from a mockingly blue sky, turning the landscape into a shimmering fairy land with color dancing across the ice crystals.

"How exactly are we going to walk through all…" I waved a hand at the leavings of the snowpocalypse. "…this?"

He laughed. "We will manage."

After a quick stop by the woodshed, where he grabbed a handsaw and two sets of snowshoes, we traipsed off the beaten path into the snow-covered backyard. Snowshoeing looked all romantic like a holiday card, but it was actually a lot more like sweaty, nasty torture. This being my first winter in Montana, I wasn't exactly used to it yet.

The white expanse narrowed down to a path leading into the one hundred wooded acres that surrounded both the cabin and the lake behind it. Sweet pine and the distinct scent of fresh snow mingled in a way that made me smile despite the seemingly impossible task before us. So much snow covered everything I could only catch glimpses of green from within the tree-shaped white giants towering on either side of the path. Under the canopy, traveling became easier since the snow wasn't quite so deep in most places.

I found a sort of rhythm with the snowshoes, and we started to make decent progress. The cool air, natural scents, and beautiful landscape soon eased the tension from my shoulders that had been building there all month. While stealing glimpses of the sexy Viking at my side, I caught him stealing glimpses of me. We smiled at each other and laughed.

"So do you have any trees in mind?" I asked after a while.

Lighting up like a holiday wreath, he nodded and pointed. "How about that one?"

Off to the right of the path, a perfectly shaped blue spruce rose up to a height of at least ten feet. Too perfect. The thought of cutting it down caused a pang to stab through my heart. "No," I said.

"How about this one?" he pointed to a fir tree on the other side of the path.

I could smell if from here and knew it would smell even more amazing in the cabin. Still, at easily over twelve feet, I hated to think of how long it took it to grow that tall.

I shook my head.

We kept looking, walking deeper into the forest, Ty pointing out perfect trees and me nixing them. They grew, lived, and breathed, and the thought of cutting any of them down wounded me. But how could I tell Ty when he seemed so excited? After easily twenty suggestions, he narrowed his gaze at me and put the handsaw down. He took his coat off, folded it, and put it beside the saw. The snowshoes came next, followed by his boots and socks.

"What are you doing?" I asked, voice going a bit high.

"Getting you out of your head." He took his shirt off, exposing his broad, muscular chest. My gaze went to the faint line of blond hair leading from his inny belly button to the top of his jeans.

"I'm sorry, what?" I asked, a bit dazed.

"You are thinking too much. You need to get back in touch with your instincts." He unzipped his jeans and pulled them down. Unaffected by the freezing temperatures like mere mortal men, his half hard cock sprung free. My mouth watered at the sight.

Oh, I was getting in touch all right.

I took a step toward him, but he held up his hand. "Strip," he said, with a mixture of suggestion and maddeningly sexy force.

All but tearing my jacket off, I hurried to comply while shooting him a sly grin. He bent to unbuckle my snowshoes, giving me a really nice view of his naked ass. I stepped out of the snowshoes and started to work on my boots. Close enough I felt his body heat, he rose before me and started unbuttoning my red flannel shirt. Ever so slowly, he pushed it off my shoulders and slid it down my arms. His fingers brushing along my bare skin made goose bumps rise in their wake. When he untucked my green undershirt from my jeans, I clenched my bottom lip between my teeth so hard I feared I might draw blood.

Our gazes met and caught like magnets. My shirt hit the pile of my other clothes. Cool air danced across my skin, but my werewolf metabolism kicked in and kept me more than warm enough. Ty moved in closer, his hands going around me. With a deft little pinch, he unclipped my bra. Moving at that same, maddeningly slow pace, he slid the straps from my shoulders and tossed the black lace and satin aside. That cold air kissed my nipples and made them stand at attention. They ached for Ty's touch.

The possibility of the snow melting right out from beneath me suddenly seemed like a real concern.

Rather than close the distance between us, he stepped back. Before I could protest, his body started to vibrate, then he shifted, his form flowing like water from that of a man into a wolf. The blond, grey, and white canine standing four feet tall at the shoulder looked every bit as muscular and formidable as his human form.

"Ty!" I complained.

My desire was so strong, I had little choice but to shift as well. Werewolves were driven to be in the form their mate took, almost uncontrollably so when aroused. And I was well and truly aroused. I shifted into a wolf and nipped at his shoulder in a playful reprimand. He chuffed, the werewolf equivalent of a laugh. Head lifting high, I turned and took off down the path, making sure to smack him across the face with my fluffy black tail.

Seemingly defying all laws of physics, the snow posed no problem to us as wolves. Our large paws allowed us to travel on the surface, working as their own sort of snowshoe. The fact we traveled on four legs, distributing our weight probably didn't hurt either. Okay, so I knew nothing of the laws of physics. While I had studied medicine in college, the science part of it had never been my thing. Hence, a change into the psychology field. While I hadn't finished my doctorate and didn't practice, the classes helped hone the skills I needed to be the seeker, so all that time wasn't a total loss.

Cool air filled my nostrils and danced through my fur, bringing with it a multitude of wonderful scents that pulled me from my incessant thinking. I opened my jaws to draw in more of it, to taste the wintery forest on my tongue and let it coat my throat. With each step I took as a wolf, more of the stress I constantly carried stripped away. Soon, I ran alongside Ty with a spring in my step, the weight of the world gone, for now at least. We traveled along the trail that went out to the lake. The towering pines draped in their cloaks of white gave way to an open expanse of smooth pearlescence beneath which the lake hid. A month ago the entire thing had frozen over solid enough to walk across, and now fresh snow topped it. We paused for a moment on a hill that overlooked it.

Ty rubbed his head along mine. I leaned into him, breathing deep of his musky wolf scent, allowing it to fill me with contentment. The incredible warmth of his body burned against mine like a furnace, one I never wanted to move away from. He gave me a wolfy smile then promptly licked the side of my face. Shaking my snout, I let out a chuffing noise, then pulled away, turned, and bolted.

With a deep bark, Ty gave chase.

Delighting in our effortless flight across the snow, the cool air filling my lungs, I scarcely noticed the five-mile run back. And running was *so* not my thing, even in wolf form. Once upon a time, I'd jogged in college, but that had been before my metabolism burned hotter than the sun, thereby eliminating the need. Most of my seeking was done at a slow hunter's pace. It involved a lot more hiking than chasing. Breathing heavy, I collapsed in the snow beside my clothes.

I rolled onto my back and shifted to human form. The cold snow felt amazing on my bare back and legs. It leached the heat of our run slowly from me. As Ty's big blond wolf burst through the brush at a run, his body flowed from that of a wolf to a man—just in time for him to land over me. Hands to either side of my head and feet outside of mine, he hovered inches above me, suspended in a sort of pushup. How on Helheimr he did such a thing in snow, I had no idea.

Loose and free breasts rising and falling with my heaving breaths, I gasped out, "You've got to possess some kind of extra magic you aren't telling me about."

His full lips twisted into an adorable smirk. "No. Just years of practice being stealthy."

Unable to not touch him, I ran my hands over his hard pectorals. "And the two hours a day you hit the gym," I pointed out.

Wiggling a brow at me, he lowered his body onto mine. The contrast of his searing skin and the cold snow beneath me felt amazing. And the pressure of his very hard erection against my legs made me gasp.

He leaned close, lips inches from mine. "Considering how hard you get my blood pumping, I guess I could cut back on the gym," he said. The husky tone of his voice made heat burn between my legs where I ached to have him.

"Yes, hard," I murmured.

Our lips crashed together in a frenzy. Tongues hungrily pursuing one another, we melded, his hands going behind my head and neck, mine exploring his back. The sensation of the cool winter air mixed with how his chest rubbed against my nipples made them so hard they ached. I reached down to grip his rock-hard ass with both hands, pulling his pelvis against me. His erection teased me, close to my sex, but my legs were pressed together too tightly to allow him entrance. The way his powerful thighs lay to either side of mine trapped me so I couldn't move. I grunted with frustration and dug my nails into his buttocks a little.

Laughing, he pulled back from our kiss. "Is there something you want, my Seeker?"

I darted forward and nipped at his neck. "You know there is." Unable to reach anything else, I sucked and bit at the skin near his collarbone.

"You're going to have to say it."

Our gazes locked, and I knew from the mischievousness I saw there he was going to make me work for it. Never one to give in, I said, "It."

Making a clucking noise, he shook his head at me. "That will not do. Naughty seekers do not get their way."

He leaned down and kissed me chastely on the lips. I groaned a complaint. His kisses trailed down my neck, around my left breast, oh so close to the needy nipple, then over to the other breast. Hot tongue darting out to wet my skin, he circled that one as well. I grew so wet I could smell my own arousal. Hovering over a breast, he looked up at me, blue eyes blown out with desire. Ever so slowly, he closed the distance, maintaining eye contact the entire time. When his mouth finally closed on my nipple, a little cry erupted from me. His tongue flicked around it before he sucked and pulled.

I lost my grip on his ass when my back bowed to press my breast further into his mouth. The weight of his body rose off mine. He picked me up and pulled me onto his lap. To my disappointment, his cock was trapped against his stomach. Denied what I truly desired, I claimed his mouth in a demanding kiss, tongue thrusting inside. I squirmed against him, marking him with my wetness. The sound of need he made caused a laugh of triumph to burst from me.

He broke the kiss. "Naughty, naughty Seeker," he murmured against my neck as he kissed me.

Before I knew it, he had flipped me over and set me on my hands and knees. Melted from our heat, a crust of snow had formed that withstood my weight. I had no time to wonder if it would hold. Ty's hot tongue licked along my seam from behind, drawing another cry from me. He groaned his approval. That tongue played maddeningly with my outer labia, finally slipping inside when I rocked back against him. He withdrew and gave my ass a little, playful slap.

"Ah, ah, ah. You have to say what you want," he reprimanded.

"I want your tongue inside me," I said without hesitation.

He complied immediately. The warm, soft pressure of his tongue slid into me so fast it made me throw my head up and call out his name loud enough to startle two birds from the tree we knelt beneath. His tongue moved in and out in a slow rhythm that made me want to weep and scream at the same time. Fingers touched my clit, massaging and circling. My breath came faster and faster in time with his talented appendages. Pressure built inside me almost instantly. I rocked back and forth against his tongue. Seconds later, my world burst apart, and my vaginal channel convulsed.

"Now put that beautiful cock of yours inside me," I demanded.

"Your wish is my command, my Seeker," he said in the sexiest voice I'd ever heard.

Cool air teased my burning sex as he withdrew. A moment later, his cock pressed at my entrance, then he filled me. We moved together slowly at first, though it killed me to do so. We both rose up on our knees, and his hands explored me from my sex to my breasts and up to cradle my face. He turned it toward him and kissed me slow and deep, all the while moving inside me. How he withstood this wonderful torture so long, I had no idea.

Tongue licking at his lips, I told him, "Come for me, hard."

The fire in his eyes threatened to burn down the forest despite the six feet of snow. A huge grin spread across his face. His pace increased tenfold. The friction combined with his growing arousal got me there again. We exploded as one. He cried out my name along with a few expletives in Icelandic.

He spooned me against him and laid us down on our sides. Making a contented noise, he nuzzled his nose through my long, black hair until it touched my neck.

"Oh woman, you undo my control in the best possible way," he said.

An almost snorting laugh erupted from me. "You could do with a bit less control."

Arms wrapping tighter around me, he cradled my right breast so it wasn't laying against the snow. "Me? This coming from the person who cleaned our cabin no less than five times from top to bottom?"

I did an awkward, one-shoulder shrug. Considering the heat that rushed to my face, I was glad he wasn't facing me. "I just want things to be perfect."

The hot breath on my neck contrasted nicely to the freezing snow against my side.

"Well, I do not," he said. "I want things to be messy and real, like us."

Those words threatened to melt not just the snow beneath me, but maybe even all the snow in Montana. I turned to face him, intent on kissing him again and probably delaying us another hour. But then I saw it. My face must have lit up because he gave me a questioning look.

I pointed behind him. "That's it. That's the perfect tree."

9

It was not the perfect tree. Seeing it up in the cabin's foyer in the morning light the next day made that painfully clear. In the tree's defense, last night when Ty and I decorated it, we had a few holiday stouts between us. And we got distracted decorating each other. It did not help that my budget only allowed for a handmade—and poorly so, considering my lack of crafting skills—popcorn garland. We'd made it last night, which, again, didn't help. Ty had created a few cute wooden squirrels, hedgehogs, and chess-piece looking idols representing the Norse Gods out of wood and pinecones for ornaments, but my attempts to duplicate them ended up looking rabid and Van Gogh-esque in a bad way.

Somehow, the decorations accentuated every gap and irregularity in the twenty-foot-tall Douglas fir. I was trying to be stealthy and move my decorations around to the back of the tree by the staircase when Ty popped around the corner from the kitchen with fir bough remnants and red ribbon in hand.

"Hey, what are you doing?" he asked, one eye narrowed at me in suspicion.

Tears started to cloud my vision. I blinked them away with a fury that surprised me. "I'm trying to fix it. We were drunk when we decorated it, and it shows." My voice caught, and I felt myself slipping closer to panic.

The scent of trees, spice, and eggnog swirled around me as Ty approached. He dropped the bough remnants and slid his arms around my waist. "My dear Sonya, we are werewolves. It would take an entire keg to get us drunk."

Ignoring the fact he was right, I twisted in his arms and continued to fuss with the tree. "Then maybe it's the tree's revenge for us murdering it."

Taking hold of my hands, he turned me gently to him. "It was a sacrifice to the Gods, a noble death, and after Yule, we will burn it to honor Balder, then plant a new tree in the new year."

Breath coming in short gasps, I pushed back a bit from him. "You'll wrinkle my top." I'd worn my best silky gold wrap blouse and a pair of black slacks I'd bought just for today. "Let go, Ty. They'll be here in less than an hour, and we're not ready." I sounded as desperate as I felt, but I couldn't help it.

Eyes closing, Ty nodded. "Ah, I see." He took my hand and led me to the bench beside the tree.

We sat down together, and I fought the urge to put my head between my knees and breathe. "You do?" I asked, having no idea what he meant.

His blue eyes captured my gaze and calming energy wrapped around my body. "I do. And you do not have to worry. My parents are going to love you. They have no expectations, I promise. More importantly, their opinion of you will not change my opinion of you or my love for you."

"What if they hate me?"

"Impossible."

My gaze narrowed. "But what if they do?"

"Then I will ask them to leave and not come back until they have come to their senses."

I straightened in surprise. "You would do that?"

Blond bangs fell across his eyes as he nodded. "Absolutely. But I will not have to. They are going to love you." He lifted one of my hands and kissed the back of it. "Sonya, this is your home now, too, as much as it is mine. They will see you as family."

A long, shuddering breath blew from me of its own accord. "I haven't had a family holiday since my dad died years ago."

Eyes closing slowly in realization, he nodded. "Well, you have nothing to worry about. I will be by your side the entire time, and no one, not even my parents, is allowed to upset you in any way, or they will suffer my wrath."

The humming sound I made low in my throat elicited a smile from him. "In that case, I'm golden, because surely, no one wants to test the wrath of a direct descendant of the thunder god," I teased as I ruffled a hand in his cheek-length blond hair.

Expression turning serious, he shook his head. "Actually my family traces our origins back to Geri, one of the wolves of Odin, not—"

I put a finger to his lips to halt his words. "I was kidding. Sort of." In appreciation of how magnificent his royal blue shirt draped over the muscles of his chest, I ran a hand down his pectorals. "Though you certainly look the part."

He gave me a full-on eyeroll that made me laugh. But then he grabbed a tiny box wrapped in red and green from under the tree, the size and shape of which made my heart stutter.

"Before they get here, I wanted to give you this," he said.

The only thing that kept me from swallowing my tongue was how he placed the box in my hand instead of something crazy like getting down on a knee.

"Open it," he pressed, eyes wide and bright with a child-like eagerness.

It took all my concentration to keep my hands from quaking as I meticulously unwrapped it, sliding a nail under each piece of tape carefully. I didn't do it to torture him so much as out of fear of what might lay inside. It wasn't that I didn't want to marry Ty, it just hadn't occurred to me that he might think we were in that place. Within the tiny box nested another tiny box, this one plush, blue velvet. My heart stopped, then started again with the force of a mule kick.

I held my breath and opened the box. On top of a bed of velvet sat a silver pendant formed of Norse knots in the shape of a crescent moon with a raven sitting on it.

Ty leaned close. "To me, the raven represents Hugin and Munin. And it seemed perfect for you because I feel as though you see me and hear me like no one else in my life ever has."

Tears I hadn't even known were forming spilled from my eyes.

He reached up and gently wiped a tear from my cheek. "I hope those are happy tears."

Swallowing the lump in my throat, I nodded furiously. "They definitely are." I handed the necklace to him, turned around, and lifted my hair out of the way. "Will you help me put it on?"

Taking the ends of the silver chain, he moved behind me and draped it around my neck. Hot breath on the sensitive skin near my ear sent delightful chills through me. The cool metal of the necklace settled just above my breasts. I reached down and traced the shape of the knotwork moon and raven. Ty's lips brushed my neck. I opened my mouth to ask how long it would be before his parents arrived when the doorbell rang.

Adrenalin hit me like a shot of top shelf Bruichladdich—which one should never shoot. Fast enough to cause whiplash if I'd been human, I flew to my feet, eyes wide, hands wringing. Ty pressed a kiss to my forehead and mouthed the words, "They will love you." I didn't even try to paste on a smile as he went and opened the door—it would have only ended up looking like a Halloween mask parody.

Seemingly oblivious to my discomfort—or more likely, politely ignoring—Ty's mom blew into the room like a hurricane of cheer. The blue-green aura of power about her felt maternal and supportive. She smelled of roses and pine needles. All smiles, she swept toward me with open arms. As a sometimes hugger, I didn't exactly panic, but I couldn't stop from freezing in place. My family had never been the sort to display affection very freely. After squeezing all the air from my lungs, she held me at arms' length and took a long look at me. Ten pounds or so of wheat colored hair piled atop her head in an artful messy bun pinned with gold hair sticks, and laugh lines danced with the crow's feet at the corners of her eyes, the only indicators that she might be over thirty-five—though I knew in truth she was well over a hundred. She wore a silky red dress that for anyone other than a werewolf would be far too light for the weather.

"Sonya, I hope it is all right that I call you Sonya?" she asked with a lovely lilt I'd come to know as an Icelandic accent.

"Yeah, of course. I'm not sure what else you would call me."

She rubbed my arms and shot a look over her shoulder at her husband. "You hear that, Viðar? She is so humble!"

I smiled and shrugged.

Giving her a nod, Viðar took her place to bend his six-and-a-half-foot frame over and wrap me in another breath-stealing hug. While he wasn't quite as broad and muscular as his son, it was clear the apple hadn't fallen far from the tree. Unlike Ty, the man sported a sexy, short beard and kept his hair almost equally short. While the orange and red aura of power around him looked a bit ominous, it felt warm and protective.

Ty introduced us. "Sonya, the man suffocating you is my father, Viðar Garrisson. This lovely woman is my mother, Betzý Edvinsdóttir. Mom, Dad, this is Sonya Michaelson."

A relieved breath eased from me when he didn't introduce me as the "Seeker of Shifterkind". It wasn't how I wanted his parents to see me.

"All right, all right, Viðar, unhand the poor girl," Betzý said.

After one more quick squeeze, Viðar did as he was told.

His wife patted him on the shoulder as if he weren't a two-hundred-pound werewolf. "Be a dear and grab my bags while Sonya and I chat?" she asked in a voice that brokered no argument despite how sweet it came across.

Inclining his head, he turned to do as she asked. With a smile, she promptly smacked him on the ass and made an appreciative humming sound. Viðar shot her a wink over his shoulder.

"Mom, no, ugh. By Odin, must you do that in front of Sonya?" Ty asked with a groan.

A laugh erupted from me. Betzý smiled and winked at me before answering her mortified son. "Clearly, Sonya is not bothered by public displays of affection."

One of Ty's pale brow's rose. "Really, mom? A kiss, a hug...those are public displays of affection. What you just did is considered harassment in at least twelve countries."

"It makes you uncomfortable that your father and I still enjoy frequent sex?" she asked, her serious tone mixed with her overly innocent expression making it clear she was enjoying the hell out of messing with him.

"Mother! Ugh!"

She waved him off. "Be a dear boy and help your father with the bags."

Grumbling beneath his breath, Ty shot me an apologetic look and swiftly followed his dad out the door.

Mouth open wide, Betzý did a bit of a spin as she stepped further inside and took in all the decorations. I bit my lip until she turned back around and I saw the expression on her face—awe, not disgust or contempt like I'd been expecting. Her eyes shone with moisture as her gaze caught mine.

"Tyler has not decorated for years, not since…" Her words trailed off.

"Since Didrik was killed," I finished for her, surprise lacing my voice. His old alpha, the one who's toppling had made Ty leave his pack and become a lone wolf. "I didn't know," I whispered. Not once had Ty given me any impression that he was sad or bothered by decorating, quite the opposite. He had leaped into it with an excited fervor that I couldn't help but get swept up into.

"Thank you for bringing joy back into my son's life." The tears cleared in a blink. "Now that they are gone, shall we have us some girl time?" she asked, brandishing a six pack of something called *Jólabjór* that looked suspiciously like a tasty brown ale.

My smile widened. "I think we're going to get along fabulously."

Laughing, she looped an arm through mine and escorted me to the kitchen. She removed two bottles of beer from the six pack and put the rest in the fridge. "Do you prefer to drink right out of the bottle, or a glass?" she asked.

"Bottle, please."

She popped the top off one and handed it to me before turning to the cabinets. Hand hovering over the door of the upper left one, she asked, "Do you still keep the glasses in here?"

"Oh, um, yeah, he does." I cringed at how awkward I sounded.

She opened the cabinet, took out a glass, and poured her beer into it. Blond brows rising, she took a sip of her beer. She sat down on the bar stool beside me and met my gaze full on. "You do not live together yet?"

Her astuteness almost made me groan, but I held the impulse in check, not wanting to offend her. I'd been hoping this conversation wouldn't happen. So much for holiday miracles. Thanks for giving me false expectations, author Wren Michaels.

In preparation for this very conversation, I'd already decided to go with the truth. "No. I'm not quite ready to give up my independence."

To my utter surprise, she patted my arm. "Good for you. Young ones are in such a hurry now days. You have centuries, so there is no rush. Of course I hope it will not take more than a few decades…" She winked and took another drink of her beer.

Stress eased out of me on my next breath. I lifted the beer to my nose. Notes of caramel and coffee drifted up to entice me. A bit less apprehensive, I took a sip. Dense but with a good balance of body, it went down surprisingly smooth.

"This is pretty good," I said, impressed.

"I am glad you like it. Tyler let me know you are a bit of a connoisseur. You tend bar, yes?"

I loved how she sounded excited by this instead of judgmental. Most people that heard how close I was to finishing my medical degree, and chose to tend bar instead weren't exactly accepting of the fact—my own mother included. And then there was the fact I was terrified Betzý would want more for her son than a bartender, even one who was the seeker.

"Yes, but I don't always plan to," I began.

"Do you enjoy it?" she asked.

The question made me really stop and think. "I do," I admitted, surprising myself. "It's a lot like being a therapist, only in a relaxed setting where the patient gets to feel like a person instead of a bug under a microscope." Damn. I hadn't meant to say that much. I filled my trap with beer. The last thing I wanted was for Ty's mom to know about my teen years spent in therapy we couldn't afford, and that hadn't worked.

"Well then, if you love it, and you are doing good for others, why do something else?" she asked.

Though it might come across as challenging to some *varúlfur*, I couldn't help but stare at her. "I um...I just thought..." Words failed me.

"You thought you had to fulfill everyone else's expectations." The gentle but blunt words made me meet her blue-eyed gaze. Before I could even scrounge up a single word of reply, she went on. "You thought because you spent years in college for a particular profession you would be wasting your time if you did not do something with it."

I nodded. "Yeah."

She leaned in close. "My dear, I can think of no better way to utilize all that psychology training than being the seeker. Just because someone doesn't pay you for it, does not make it any less important." Sitting back up, she slapped a hand on her leg. "So why not tend bar in your off time if you love it?"

I'd never thought of it that way, and I certainly hadn't imagined anyone else ever would. Grinning, I picked my beer up and raised it toward her. "I like how you think Betzý."

She clinked her glass to my beer and we drank to it. I wasn't quite sure what I'd been expecting, but this amazing woman was certainly not it. For once, I was glad I'd been wrong.

10

By the time the guys came back in the setting sun was stretching golden rays inside the huge picture windows facing the peekaboo view of the lake. The room seemed to glow, turning our scraggly looking tree into something unique and beautiful.

Ty's dad slapped his hands together and rubbed them vigorously, excitement lighting up his eyes. "Are you ladies up for some caroling before we open our *Jólabókaflóðið* gifts, what do you say?"

The grin fell from Ty's face and tension sang through his power.

"Yes! That sounds wonderful!" Betzý exclaimed.

Swallowing so hard I could see his throat working, Ty stepping abruptly to my side and put an arm around me. "I am not sure about that. Sonya isn't familiar with our traditions."

Viðar waved a hand and made a scoffing sound. "No time like the present to introduce her then," he proclaimed, shooting me a wink.

I gave him a smile in return. "Sure, why not?" Though I didn't see how caroling could be a *varúlfur* tradition. Unless the songs were completely different, it didn't track with Odinism. But that could explain Ty's hesitation. I patted his back. "I can just hum along if I don't know the tune," I assured him.

"About that…" he whispered.

"Excellent! Shall we start with your friends, Ayra and Vidar? I would love to see them." She patted Ty on the cheek, which might have been one of the cutest things I'd ever seen. "Your father and I were so excited to hear about their mating."

"Mom! By Thor, could you use a different word?" he whispered.

Laughter slipped from me as we made our way to the front door. I loved seeing him like this.

"Ah my little Tyler, always the shy one. The stories I could tell you, Sonya—"

"Mom, you absolutely will not," Ty interrupted.

While they chatted Viðar slipped into the kitchen and grabbed the plate of cookies off the bar. He winked at me when he returned. "For the road," he whispered in a conspiratorial tone.

"I'd love to hear them," I told Betzý.

Eyes brightening, she looped an arm through mine. "Wonderful! Tales for the road, then."

Ty groaned, making me laugh.

We piled into his parents' short bed, four door, green, pickup truck. At first glance I thought it an odd choice for *varúlfur*, but then Viðar turned the engine over and I realized it was an electric vehicle. True to her word, Ty's mom regaled us with all manner of cute, funny, and embarrassing stories about him during the two hour drive up to Hemlock Hollow. His childhood sounded amazing and completely opposite of mine, which at least partially explained why he had his act together so much more than I did. Rather than intimidate me like I thought it would, though, it made me happy to know he'd grown up so loved and supported.

Ty's dad handled the snow and ice of Montana roads in December like it was nothing, which I guess it wasn't to him since he'd lived between here and Iceland all of Ty's life. The safe, confident way he drove the vehicle allowed me to relax and enjoy the adorable flush of pink coloring Ty's cheeks. Aside from half-hearted protests, he took it all in stride. He laughed at himself. I loved that about him.

Before I knew it we were on the road traveling through the wolf preserve that surrounded Hemlock Hollow. Just as I started to wonder about Ty's protest regarding caroling, Viðar pulled the truck into a paved turnaround with a view. The snow-covered mountains looked close enough to touch. I was still laughing at the latest story Betzý had told when we stepped out of the vehicle.

That laughter died abruptly when she and Viðar removed their shoes, promptly followed by their shirts. One flick of her fingers and Betzý removed her bra. Wide-eyed, I turned to Ty.

"I tried to tell you. They do not mean the human tradition of caroling, but the *varúlfur* one."

Before I could formulate any words, his parents had stripped off the remainder of their clothes and stood naked in the snow at the front of the truck. Relief over not having to see the rest of them naked warred with indignation over Ty not having prepared me for this. I glared at him, hard.

"It is not too late to back out," he said.

Giving him a tight smile, I took my blouse off, then reached for the button of my jeans. "Oh no, I am not backing out," I assured him.

The only way for me to learn more about his culture, about *varúlfur* culture, was to experience it. And I wasn't about to disappoint his parents if I could help it. Cold air danced across my naked skin as I set my clothes in the truck. My *varúlfur* metabolism kicked in and raised my core temperature until it felt comfortable.

Two unnaturally large blond-gray wolves played in the snow near the stone wall of the overlook. They swiped pawfuls of snow at one another, chuffing and barking. When Ty stepped up beside me naked and oh-so-yummy looking, a smile had spread across my face.

"This will be fun, I promise," he said. As the last word left his lips, his body shimmered, then flowed from the form of a man into that of a wolf.

I shifted a moment later and together we ran to join his parents. With Viðar in the lead, the four of us took off at jog down a trail that led into the trees. Clean, snow-scented air filled my expanding lungs as we loped along. Even in the silence of the winter night, our paws scarcely made a sound against the soft, newly fallen snow. Ty's parents ran side by side, throwing huge wolfy grins at each other every now and then. Love all but pulsed through their power. It was a beautiful thing to see.

In a few miles, we crossed from the preserve into Hemlock Hollow. A short lope over an open meadow of sparkling white, and we reached the edge of the forest that bordered Ayra and Vidar's land. A light dusting of snow began to fall when we approached their cabin. Unsure of what exactly we were doing, I hung back with Ty and waited.

His parents stopped near the back deck, sat down, and began to howl. After a look at me, Ty joined in. For a moment I could only stare in shock. But the sound pulled at something deep inside me. My wolf side wanted to join. The human side of me feared sounding like a dying cow. Wolfy things were not things I was good at. But as a human I could carry a tune good enough. Hoping that translated to being a wolf, I tipped my head up and let out a howl. It didn't sound half bad. I followed along, mimicking the cadence of Ty and his parents' voices.

After a few moments, the French doors leading onto the back deck opened and Ayra and Vidar stepped out. Wrapped in a fluffy green robe, long, white-blond hair loose about her, Ayra looked a bit sleepy. But the huge grin on her face told me she didn't mind the interruption. Vidar came up alongside her and put an arm around her as he peered out at us. When our song ended, he cocked his head.

"By Odin's beard, Sonya and Ty? Is that you?" he asked.

Ty gave a little yip which I echoed. He followed it up with a growly, barking noise that I didn't even attempt to emulate. I had no idea what he said and I didn't want to try it and end up inadvertently saying something rude about Vidar's mom or something. Whatever it was he'd said made Vidar turn to Ayra with a hopeful smile. Lips pursed, she stared at him for a moment. Eventually she caved beneath the power of his puppy dog eyes and nodded. She and Vidar walked back inside. We waited. Not quite understanding why, I gave Ty a curious look. In return he gave me a huge, wolfy grin.

A moment later, Vidar and Ayra emerged naked. Before I could even look away, they leaped over their second story deck, shifted as they fell, and hit the snow as wolves—Ayra's white as winter and Vidar's dark as a starless night. Like a couple of excited canines, Ty and Vidar jogged circles around each other, leaping up, biting, tails wagging. Ayra and I just nodded at each other like sane creatures. The hint of a smile tugged at the side of her mouth.

Led by Betzý, we sent a chorus of howls up to the new moon. Before it could become a full-on song, she and Ty's dad led the way to our next destination. We spent easily two more hours visiting their friends, and we even dropped by where Candice was staying to sing for her. By the time we returned to the truck I was exhausted and hoarse, but happier than I could remember being during the holiday in a long time.

After we got home, the four of us spent several hours chatting, drinking *Jólabjór*, and eating *piparkökur*—Icelandic holiday cookies similar to gingersnaps. With their playful, laid-back attitudes, his parents were easy to be around. They treated me like family instead of a Gods-chosen super-werewolf. It was refreshing.

Eyes wide with excitement, Ty's mom rose from the barstool. "Time for *Jólabókaflóðið*. Shall we?"

I rose too. "After all those cookies and beer, I could use a good read by the fire," I said.

Ty and Viðar grabbed for the last of my cookies at the same time and promptly fell into a wrestling competition that made me fear for the dishes on the bar top. Shaking her head at them and grinning, Betzý looped an arm through mine again as we walked toward the L-shaped couch standing before the fireplace. Flames licked at the wood Ty had strategically piled inside, casting a golden glow on the metal family crest that lined the back of the fireplace.

"Guess my cookies weren't that bad," I said.

Betzý patted my hand before letting go and claiming a spot on the couch. "They were delicious, dear. I do hope you will share the recipe with me."

I settled into my favorite spot closest to the fireplace. "Of course," I said.

After a few more clangs and bangs from the kitchen, the guys came in, each with presents in one hand and half a cookie in the other. Gracing me with a gorgeous grin, Ty's dad handed me a book-shaped present, then sat down and wrapped an arm around his wife. I plucked at the natural material of the pretty red bow, reluctant to damage it. My heart rate ratcheted up when Ty handed his parents the presents I had picked out for them. Suddenly, I doubted my choices. *What if I got it wrong and they are forced to read a terrible book all night?* That would be a great first impression to make.

Sensing my discomfort, Ty sat down beside me, picked one of my hands up, and kissed the back of it. The warmth of his breath sped my heart for a completely different reason. Soothing energy flowed from him to me, allowing me to breathe easier.

We tore into our presents, me a bit slower because I wanted to see their reaction to the present I'd gotten them.

An interesting 'squee' noise came from Ty's mom. "*A Kingdom of Deceit and Desire*. Oh Sonya, you know how to pick them. I love Leslie O'Sullivan! I did not know she had another book in this series out."

"You really like her?" I asked.

"Absolutely. Viðar and I will just have to retire to our room when I get to the sexy part," she said as she wiggled her eyebrows.

Ty groaned. "You might literally be killing me, mom."

We laughed, Ty even joining in after a moment. The rest of us opened our books and dug in. Soon, the only sound in the cabin was the crackling of the fire. Tucked into the couch beside Ty, surrounded by the warmth of his family, I couldn't imagine a better holiday—filled with the magic of both books and belonging.

PART TWO

AYRA'S STORY

1

KERTASNÍKER

I hadn't been forced to kill anyone in two weeks, and I was getting twitchy. But that wasn't the only reason I was doing shadow yoga on our back deck in eighteen-degree weather. Yule was in full swing and Vidar's parents had invited us over for the Wild Hunt.

It wasn't like they were horrible. Horrible I could deal with. I'd grown up with it and was as used to it as breathing. The problem was, they were the varúlfur version of the American Dream family and I was anything but. I was the reaper of shifterkind, tasked by Odin to kill any shifter who lost their battle with madness and became a murderer. Not exactly 'take home to the parents' material.

It helped, of course, that they were werewolves like me and weren't averse to killing those who needed it. But they didn't go around doing it all the time like I did.

My breathing hitched and then turned into a long exhale that filled the cold air with a cloud of white. I bent deeper into my front knee in a Warrior Two pose and cast my gaze over the snow-blanketed yard behind our cabin. Pristine white hills ended at a half circle of snow-laden evergreen trees. Some of the boughs of the trees dipped so low under their burden they looked like they were on the verge of breaking. Beyond those rose white, high-peaked mountains framed by a bright blue sky. Though cold, northern Montana was beautiful in the winter.

At least six feet of snow had fallen over the last month. And there would be plenty more to come over the next three to four months.

I didn't mind. I loved the crisp air and the way the snow made everything look clean and pretty. Much like the snow, I could put on an attractive cover and hide the ugliness beneath if I needed to. Vidar's parents didn't need to see the monster I'd become. They remembered me as a comic reading little girl in braids, one who loved storms and was their youngest son's best friend. It wasn't like we had to talk about reaping. I could do this.

As I finished a sweeping movement with my arms, the pressure of the most wonderful energy on the planet approach from within the house. I felt it like spring coming, warm, inviting, and filled with life.

The French doors opened behind me with a soft click. Calming energy flowed around me, caressing my body before he even stepped foot on the deck. It seeped into me and drained away more of my anxiety than an hour of yoga had.

"Sorry to interrupt," came Vidar's deep voice. It resonated through my bones, warming me despite the sub-freezing weather.

The magnetic forces that drew us together turned me around. It was impossible not to look at him when he was near. The man was just that compelling for me.

His tall, muscular frame forced him to duck as he stepped through the doors. In black sweatpants and a black T-shirt with an artistic image of Odin's face on it, he made casual look scorching. The T-shirt was loose everywhere but across his large pectoral muscles and bulging biceps.

Barefoot, he walked across the freezing deck without any sign of flinching. But then he wouldn't. The cold didn't affect our kind like it did humans. Dark green eyes with yellow shooting out from the pupils like solar flares locked on mine as he approached. I would never get tired of staring at those amazing eyes.

He cocked his head. "I'm afraid the yoga isn't working. I can feel your tension all the way in the office," he said in deliciously rich, deep voice.

Crinkling my nose up, I looked down at the stormy sky and lightning depicted on my yoga mat. Though not an art most would choose for a relaxing practice, I loved it. Being a conduit for lightning, storms calmed me, made me feel closer to the Gods.

"Sorry about that," I said.

A dark-skinned hand interrupted my view of the mat, one finger lifting my chin. "Don't be. You don't have to be sorry for your feelings, remember?"

Our gazes locked again. In those gorgeous eyes was a strength that bolstered me. He and Sonya—both as my friend and therapist—had been working with me on not being sorry so much. I'd been programmed by my family to be sorry for my very existence, so I tended to apologize a lot. It was a very hard habit to break.

"I'm—yes. I remember. It's just that I'm nervous to attend the Wild Hunt with your parents."

Sighing, he rubbed my bare arms. His hands felt like they'd been in heated gloves. I must have gotten chilly out here in the cold. Thanks to my varúlfur constitution, I barely noticed it, though.

"Why? You've known them your whole life," he asked.

I looked away from those loving eyes. "Because I'm the uppskera now, and your girlfriend."

He pulled me against his chest and wrapped his arms around me. "You are amazing, thoughtful and sweet. They have always known that. Being the uppskera hasn't made those qualities any lesser in you."

"But I'm a killer," I mumbled against his chest.

Laughter made his chest vibrate beneath my ear. "We're varúlfur. We're all killers."

"I know, but—"

He drew away and held me at arms' length. "No buts. They love you as I do."

Grinning, I moved my hands to his hips and pulled his pelvis against me. "Not exactly as you do," I said low and sultry.

He cupped my ass and laughed again. "Very true."

One hand cradling my chin, he started to bend down to kiss me. The phone in his back pocket began to buzz and he froze. We groaned in unison. Foreheads resting together, we paused for a moment. Then he grabbed his phone out of his pocket and looked at it.

He pushed the answer button. "Hey Sonya."

I heard her answer, not because she was a loud talker, buy because of my heightened varúlfur hearing. "Is Ayra there? She isn't answering her phone?"

"Yep." Vidar handed me the phone.

Before he let me take it though, he asked. "Do you know where the candles are? I can't find them."

"In the hall closet," I said.

He shook his head. "Nope. The candle box is empty."

"Odd. It was over half full last time I took one out." I quirked a brow up. "Why, what are you planning?"

Bending, he kissed me lightly on the lips before putting the phone in my hand. "You'll have to wait and see."

I watched him walk back into the house, appreciating the way his black sweatpants curved around his ass. Later I planned to have my hands on that gorgeous posterior.

For now, I lifted the phone to my ear. "Hey Sonya."

"Sorry for interrupting," the Sköll to my Hati, the yin to my yang, and my best and only female friend in the world said.

"Don't be. Anticipation makes the mating all the more intense."

Laughter sounded from the other end of the phone. "True. Hey, listen, I need a favor."

"Anything."

"I need you to go holiday shopping with me."

Ugh. Anything but that. Were it anyone other than Sonya, I would have reneged on the 'anything' promise. But I would do anything for her, even that.

2

SKYRGÁMUR

Thankfully, we weren't going shopping for a few days. Which meant I got to relax the next morning with a good book and a bowl of oatmeal. I'd wanted skyr—a delicious Icelandic yogurt—but apparently Vidar had eaten it all because I couldn't find it anywhere in the fridge.

So I dealt with oatmeal as I read *With Shield and Ink and Bone* by Casey L. Bond. Cuddled up on the couch beside the fireplace, I was comfy and happily enthralled by my book.

But as was my lot in life, all good things were all too brief.

Halfway into chapter thirteen, an anxious, almost nauseous feeling gripped me. Dropping my ereader, I bolted upright. It was a feeling I knew well. A condemned was nearby. No, not condemned, not yet. From the level of urgency in my gut, I could tell they hadn't lost their battle with madness, but they were close to it.

I couldn't afford to ignore the feeling. Better to be get close in case they lost it and started killing people so I could stop them and put them down quick. Besides, Sonya was likely there, trying to help them, which meant she was in danger.

I was on my feet before my ereader stopped bouncing on the couch cushion. In the next beat I stood in the foyer, rummaging through a drawer in the table. I pulled a pen and paper out and wrote Vidar a quick note.

There's a troubled close to losing it nearby. I'm going to make sure they don't, and that Sonya is safe.

I knew they were close because I had to be within a few miles for the feeling to manifest.

It would be a waste of time to tell him not to wait up or come after me. If he got home before I did, he would come.

I stripped, folded my clothes, and placed them on the bottom shelf of the foyer table. Cold poured in the front door as I opened it, wrapping around my warm skin. But I barely noticed it. My body began to vibrate with the change, heating and banishing the cold as it did so.

As soon as I heard the door click closed behind me, I leaped from the deck toward the snowy front yard. I flowed from the form of a woman into that of a wolf, easy as milk pouring from a carton into a glass. White paws met the snow, the pads spreading out to help keep me on the crusty top layer.

Following that feeling in my gut, I ran toward the glistening white forest. I flowed through the snow-laden trees with ease. So as not to bring a cascade of snow down behind me, I kept my tail straight out, avoiding low-hanging branches. The pull in my gut drew me off our land and toward the southeast. I crossed the edge of the Draupnir pack territory and kept going. There was no sign or fence to tell me this. I knew by the change in the trees, the underbrush. But mostly, I knew by the feel of the land itself.

The sun moved higher into the sky. Draupnir land soon gave way to federal forest. The sun moved lower in the sky. On one paw, stepping off Hemlock Hollow property felt good, freeing. On the other, it came with the risk of hunters and ranchers who disliked wolves. But the season was wrong for hunters and snow this deep would keep poachers at home by the fire. And thankfully, the pull wasn't taking me across any lowlands where ranchers had moved their herds for the winter.

The sun set behind the mountains, painting the snow upon them pink. Darkness claimed the land and the temperature dropped.

Trotting across a ridgeline with frosty pines to the left and a cliff to my right, the pull grew so strong I knew

I was almost there. The icy ridge soon turned into a hillside, and I began to creep slowly down it.

They weren't far now, within half a mile based on the level of unease in my gut. I sensed something else besides the troubled young werewolf. A familiar energy almost as comforting as Vidar's was with them. Sonya.

I smelled them on the wind—a young, male newly bitten and a female with the spice of something special. Special was inadequate when it came to my only friend in the world besides Vidar. Chosen by the Goddess Frigg to help save troubled new werewolves from going mad, she was nothing short of spectacular.

Careful to stay hidden, I crept closer. Couldn't have the new wolf scenting me and freaking out. That would certainly ruin all Sonya's careful work with them. Still, I couldn't leave. I had to make sure she was safe. Troubled newly bitten wolves were extremely dangerous, and fighting wasn't Sonya's strong suit.

Two human figures stood a hundred or so yards away in the valley below, dark dots on the white landscape.

"I change my mind. I don't want to be a werewolf," the male said through a sob.

Sympathy sparked in me. Though I'd been born with my varúlfur side awakened and it was second nature to me, the reaper side of me was different. It had been awakened only recently, forced upon me by my brother who resented the fact I'd been chosen over him.

The newly bitten's name drifted on the breeze as he told it to Sonya. Dax. Crouching low, I moved a little closer. Thankfully, I was a white wolf and the heavy snowfall helped hide me completely.

Sonya's gentle voice responded. She sympathized with him, established a connection, and began telling him some of the positive things about being varúlfur. She invited him to go somewhere warm. They began walking.

At the base of the hill I crept down, to the west slightly, a cave gaped. The snow had been beaten down with footprints leading up to it. They walked inside and soon the orange and yellow glow of a fire lit the dark opening.

The full moon was two nights away, which meant she had time to work with him. But it wouldn't be easy. Tomorrow it would be full enough to affect him. By the feel of his power, I could tell the guy hadn't shifted yet. But he'd been bitten, which awakened the power that lay dormant in his blood. He was stronger now, faster, and more instinctual. Add fear to that and it could be an explosive combination.

If he failed to control his wolf and his instincts and went mad, I'd have to put him down. But she had from now until the night after the full moon to work with him. If he didn't endanger her beyond what she could handle, they'd never know I was here. But if he did, he'd learn why all of shifterkind feared me.

I settled down onto the snow beneath a cedar tree to watch and wait.

Sonya put her psychologist skills to good use chatting with the newly bitten through most of the night. I slept through a lot of it. He wouldn't shift tonight, so she was safe. Best to get my rest when I could. They slept through half the next day, leaving me nothing to listen to but the crackling of the fire Sonya had built.

Finally, I heard Sonya stir. When she returned to the cave after taking care of her morning business, I crept out from beneath the cedar boughs where I could see better. She was messing with her phone. I focused on my hearing, honing it in and amplifying it with my power.

The subzero air helped carry her voice to me. "Hey gorgeous. Thanks for the clothes and supplies."

I couldn't hear the response from who she was talking to. Chances were she had the phone turned down because she didn't need it very loud. Sharp hearing was a thing for our kind. But hers was exceptional even among varúlfur. Which was part of why I was being extremely quiet and keeping my distance.

From what she was saying it was clear she was talking to her boyfriend Ty. And it sounded like he was going to come out and keep an eye on her. Which gave me a pass for two days. He would keep her safe and was far less likely to spook the newly bitten than I was if he scented me.

I could return to my book and bed for two nights. If I needed to come back, my gut would tell me. Still, knowing someone else would keep her safe and doing it myself were too very different things. She was a bright, amazing person that our kind needed as much as they needed air. And she was my only female friend.

The enticing scents of bacon and eggs cooking made me hyper aware of how empty my stomach was. Snout lifting to inhale as much of it as I could, I let my mouth gape open.

Sonya and Dax began chatting again. He sounded like a nice kid. He'd grown up knowing about our kind, knowing he was descended from them. He'd asked to be bitten in. Now, he was having second thoughts. Too bad it was far too late for that.

The soft sound of warm paws moving across the frozen crust that covered last night's new snow made my ears flick backwards. Rising onto all fours, I turned to look. Several yards away, around the reddish trunk of another cedar I spotted a huge black wolf. Green-gold eyes regarded me with patience. Vidar was just as gorgeous as a wolf as he was a man.

Glancing down at the distant cave one more time, I made my decision. While a book and my bed were tempting, a meal and the arms of my man convinced me.

3

GILJAGAUR

I'd been worried for nothing. Sonya worked her magic and had Dax shifting by the last day of the full moon without any fear of going insane. Since that meant I probably wouldn't have to kill anyone during Yule, I considered it a win for all involved.

The rapidly approaching holidays got my hackles up. Not literally at the moment, since I was in human form. But every time I shifted into a wolf it became all too literal. When I'd been a kid, the berating, beatings, and bruises always grew worse this time of year. Those days were behind me now, but their scars still pinched. I was working on releasing the trauma, but it wasn't the kind of thing only a few years out of a broken home could erase.

It didn't help that there was no milk in the fridge and the house smelled like sage. According to Vidar, the energy in the house needed cleansing. For my sensitive nose, the scent was overpowering, but I wasn't going to stomp on his spiritual practices. Thankfully I'd only mixed the dry ingredients for the gingerbread cookies. After a deep perusal of the interior of the fridge, I gave up and closed the door.

A *meow* sounded from the floor a moment before Heimdallr, my orange and white striped cat, wound around my legs. I bent down and scratched his head. Instantly a loud purr issued from him.

"Did you drink all the milk?" I asked.

He flicked his ringed tail and walked off toward his food bowl.

"I can't tell if that's a yes or no," I said through a sigh.

He stared at his empty food bowl with a forlorn expression made all the more pathetic looking by the chunk missing out of his right ear. The moment I re-opened the fridge door he perked up and let out another loud *meow*. I grabbed the specialty gourmet meat cat food and filled his bowl. After a glance at it, he started purring, then walked off. He leaped up onto the couch and nestled into the green chenille throw.

"You little Loki-touched brat! You probably did beg it all off Vidar." I walked over and scratched his head again. "Didn't you?"

The smug look he gave me suggested I was on to something. I strode down the hall, stopping at the oak table in the cubby beside the garage door to snag the keys to Vidar's Jeep.

The scent of warm wax filled my nose as I opened the garage door. The gravely voice of AC/DC filled the garage.

Beyond my motorcycle and the forest green Jeep 4XE, I could just see the top of Vidar's shorn, curly, black hair. As he scraped wax from the base of the snowboard on his workbench, he sang along with the song about being thunder struck. The sepia tank he wore gave me a delicious view of his ebony, tattooed, muscular arms as they flexed with each scrape.

The man looked so tasty I considered abandoning the baking and having a mouthful of him instead. The only thing that held me back was his excitement about our snowboarding/sking trip in a few days. His grin as he worked on our gear was nothing short of beautiful.

Faded blue jeans hugged his perfect ass as he bent over the board to scrape it. I walked up and smacked that ass. His grin grew and he lowered the volume on the speaker to his right. Scraper in hand, he turned and took me in his arms. His muscular body was all hard planes and valleys against mine. It tested my resolve to wait.

The way his green and gold eyes lit up and beamed down at me didn't help matters.

"You drank all the milk," I said through my own grin, traitorous hands snaking around his waist.

"Nope," he said in his silky, deep voice.

"Then you gave all the milk to Heimdallr."

"Nope again."

"Either you're covering for the cat's manipulative convincing, or your own gullibility."

"Still nope."

I traced a claw over one of his bulging biceps, following the knotwork lines of the tattoo there. "Sticking to your guns. I like that."

Rolling his fingers into a fist, he flexed. "You like my guns?"

Heat scoured through me, settling in my abdomen. "Very much," I said in a husky voice.

Lifting my chin, I indicated the board on the table and my skis leaned against the wall. "You done?"

"Halfway."

I released a disappointed sigh as I slid from his arms and stepped back. "In that case, I'll leave you to it and go grab some milk so I can finish the cookies."

Catching one of my hands, he pulled me back to him. "The waxing can wait."

Lips pursing and eyes narrowing, I shook my head. "But my cookies can't. I promised Fritz I'd bring them tomorrow."

He pulled me against him. "My brother doesn't need cookies."

I smacked one of his large pectoral muscles. "Yes he does. They're payment for him taking us cat skiing."

A long-suffering groan came from him. "He doesn't need payment either."

The seriousness in his tone made me look down. "I know, but I want to make them for him," I said softly.

He wound a lock of my long, white-blond hair around a finger. "All right." His other hand pulled me closer.

Folding his tall body down and bending his legs to get to my level, he pressed his full lips to mine. Our tongues met. He tasted like peppermint and ginger ale, a surprisingly delicious combination. Before I could get too lost in the amazing feel of his body pressed to mine, I broke the kiss.

"You're getting wax in my hair," I teased a bit breathlessly.

He laughed low and deep. The sound forced me to turn and start walking. If I didn't, I was going to tear his clothes off and throw him down on the bench, wax be damned.

"What shall I make you for dinner while you're out running errands?" he called after me.

Keys jingling, I waved a hand. "Nothing. You finish waxing, I'll grab take-out at Mike's."

"Oooo, yes! Be sure to get me a—"

"Pumpkin spice milkshake. I know. I wouldn't dream of forgetting," I interrupted.

He blew me a kiss as I hopped in his Jeep and started it. While I waited for the garage door to open I watched him as he bent back to his work. I daydreamed of what I'd do to that body once I got home. It was better than thinking about going into a town filled with werewolves who would grovel at my feet.

4

Once upon a time Hemlock Hollow used to be a sanctuary for me. It had been a place I could get away from my mentally abusive parents and physically abusive brother. The bookstore where Vidar and I had spent much of our childhood huddled in the comic section, the library where I'd spent hours in the secret basement supernatural shelves, the park where we'd spent hours beneath the massive spruce and Hemlock trees, all held good memories.

But the place had changed for me since I'd become the reaper of all shifterkind. All these werewolves I'd grown up alongside now showed me a reverence—and sometimes fear—that I didn't feel I warranted. Except for the fear part. I'd earned that when I killed my tyrannical brother.

Vidar had helped me convince everyone to stop leaving gifts at our cabin, but now they just tried not to charge me for any services. Which was exactly what had me grinding my teeth on the way from the grocery store to Mike's Malt shop. I'd been forced to leave cash on the counter since the cashier had refused to let me pay.

Being treated like Odin's chosen one was not for me. I didn't deserve it. Slowly, with Vidar's and Sonya's help, I was learning not to loathe myself, but I would never accept the belief that I was better than anyone else.

Not even the cheerily lit pine boughs hanging from every old-fashioned streetlamp that lined Aðal street could lift my mood. My morose eased a tiny bit as I drove around the city-block-sized roundabout that was really more of a seemingly endless corner in the center of town. The towering spruce trees in the park at its center, boughs all heavy with snow and lit up with multi-colored solar powered lights, were something to behold. It looked like a small forest all lit up with magic and I loved it. Always had. Which was part of why I'd instinctively driven this way.

I could have stayed out of the main part of town, the part Hemlock Hollow kept non-wolfy for the occasional tourist who found their way here. But I'd wanted to see it. The massive *Welcome to Hemlock Hollow* sign mounted between two towering trees to either side of the road boasted the biggest wreath likely in existence. Natural pine boughs and holly berries had been used to create it, and several members of each pack in town had helped build it. It was all lit up with white lights that made the snow covering it glow.

Magic indeed.

Just beyond the sign sat Mike's Malt shop to the left. The wood slatted A-frame building poked up out of the snow like a witch's hat adorned with colorful lights. A massive wreath of cedar boughs nestled in the sharp peak of the roof. The outdoor seating area and covered deck had both been cleared of snow. Teenagers sat around gas powered firepits beneath the massive pergola eating and chatting. Being varúlfur, they were mostly unaffected by the cold.

Vidar and I had spent many days of our childhood there. The memory brought an easy smile to my lips.

I parked the Jeep in an open spot and walked up the steps. To each side of the door Nordic skis were mounted on the wall and below them sat a pair of old ski boots decorated with green and red ribbons and sprigs of evergreen. Tiny, colorfully wrapped boxes poked up from within the boots.

The shop's adherence to such a quaint tradition pinched at a place deep in my chest.

When I was small, I left a decorated boot outside my bedroom window during Yule each year until I turned thirteen. Little gifts would show up in it each morning, sometimes roasted chestnuts, sometimes candy, sometimes books. But the winter I turned thirteen my brother beat me bloody for clinging to such childish notions. My parents only nodded and voiced their agreement that it was time I grew up. I never did it again after that.

Cheery music about snow poured from the door when I opened it. Even though it was the middle of the week, the place was filled with teenagers. Not a single table was empty. Even the second story with a balcony that overlooked the first looked packed. Yule break was in full swing. The heat of so many bodies rushed out around me.

Most of the chatter died the second I stepped over the threshold. Worse, it abruptly struck back up in hushed whispers. My varúlfur hearing picked it all up, even those on the balcony.

"That's her!"

"There she is."

"I heard she can suck the energy right out of you."

"She can suck anything out me she wants!"

"Idiot, she can kill you with a flick of her little finger."

"I heard she's killed over ten varúlfur."

"This month maybe. Overall its way more than that."

The words shouldn't have stung. Thanks to my parents and brother, I had the skin of an elephant and shark hybrid. Still, the comments dug down into me. Growing up as the kid with the mark of the uppskera had been bad enough. Now that I'd come into the power, people didn't just treat me like an oddity. They treated me like the murderer I was.

"Shut up you idiots! Her hearing is better than ours."

Some of the conversation died down after that. Energy carefully controlled, I strode to the end of the counter with the register on it. Thankfully, it was away from the bar seats filled with kids.

The tall blond teen guy behind the counter looked up with a smile that crinkled his nose and made his gold nose ring lift. That smile melted as his brown eyes fell on me. Though he didn't move an inch, I felt his power crawl away from me, retreating as far into him as it could.

"Ayra…m'am…I mean, Miss Valdisdöttir. Wha…what can I do for you?" he stuttered.

A pretty woman with a long, blond ponytail pulled high atop her head, strode up and sat two paper bags of food and two shakes on the counter. She smacked the guy on the back of the head. "Don't mind him, Ayra. He's an idiot."

I put some bills down on the counter and lifted the bag to my nose. The delicious aromas of fries and burgers slinked around me. "Thanks, Ofelia."

"You want your change?"

"Nope. That's your tip."

Winking, she blew a kiss at me. The guy with the nose ring stared gape-mouthed at her.

"He doesn't deserve it," she said as I turned away.

"Then you keep it," I said with a lift of my brows.

Though she wasn't a friend in the way of hanging out with me or being someone I could call, she'd always been nice to me. As a kid, when I'd come by the restaurant bloody from a fight with Calder, she always let me clean up in the bathroom. She had snuck me milkshakes and fries when my parents wouldn't let me eat dinner because I hadn't done well enough in training. She'd gossip to me about all the goings on in school and town. Not a friend, exactly, but someone who'd been kind when few others were.

It seemed some things didn't change and this one made me smile.

Bags of food tucked into my arms and shakes in hand, I put my back to the door and pushed it open

When I turned into the cold I nearly stepped right into a new face—one framed in chin-length, chestnut hair with an easy grin that no doubt melted teen girls' hearts. His happy-go-lucky expression doused from his face as his eyes met mine. Those eyes went wide and startled and his power quivered and retreated within him.

"Are…are…you he…here for me?" he sputtered out in a small, terrified voice that did not match his six-foot frame of youthful muscle.

Though my heart sank at his reaction, I knew my carefully schooled expression revealed nothing. I lifted the shakes in my hands. "Nope. Just dinner."

Typically I would have left it at that, walked around him, and made a quick exit. But I'd been learning from Sonya that a little conversation went a long way to mending things.

"Max, no, Dax, right?" I asked.

He nodded. "Yes, ma'am."

"Should I be here for you?" I asked, unable to resist teasing him.

Jaw tensing, he swallowed hard. "No, ma'am. I'm doing good. I'm able to shift back and forth and my kennari says there are no signs of madness."

"That's good. You like your kennari, they're doing a good job teaching you?" I asked.

"I do. They are."

The snow-coated parking lot beckoned. This conversation stuff was hard.

"Good. Sounds like you've got a handle on this, kid. You've nothing to fear from me."

A sigh blew from him, his shoulder drooped, and he relaxed so much I was afraid for a second he might faint. Thankfully, he didn't. It would have sucked to have to drop my dinner to catch him.

"Thank you, ma'am," he said with such feeling and relief that it stabbed at me.

I walked around him and went down the stairs. As he walked inside several people called out to him in greeting. "You survived!" one guy teased.

"Shut it, moron. She can still hear you!" said a female voice followed by a loud *smack*.

It would have made me smile if it didn't hurt so bad that to them I was someone to be feared and avoided—the reaper.

5

GÁTTAPEFUR

The stillness of the morning shattered with the sound of someone rifling through the cupboards. I finished my braid and tossed the plait of pale blond hair back over my shoulder. I opened the bathroom door to Heimdall who sat swishing his tail back and forth. I couldn't tell if the perturbed look on his face was because I'd closed him out of the bathroom, or because Vidar was making a racket in the kitchen.

Together the cat and I walked down the hall to go see what all the fuss was about. Vidar stood with his back to me, black base layer pants hugging his toned buttocks and legs. He had spices and other baking ingredients all over the counter. Their smells lingered with that of Vidar and the warming oven.

I sat down on a barstool, propped my elbows on the butcher block countertop, and just watched. Heimdallr jumped up on the stool to my right.

"Good morning," Vidar said without turning around. Of course he'd felt my energy as I approached. Probably the cat's too.

"Good morning. What are you doing?"

Heimdallr *meowed* at him.

He turned far enough to give me a sly smile over his shoulder. "Baking cookies."

Brows scrunching together, I got up and went to the fridge. "There should be two dozen in here," I said as I opened it.

There wasn't a cookie in sight. The container I'd had them, all ready to go for today's ski trip, was gone.

I smacked his perfect ass lightly. "V, you ate all the cookies I made for Fritz!"

He dropped the spoon he'd been using to cut the butter into the sugar with. "I didn't. I swear to the Norns." Though he sounded earnest, I had my doubts.

"Um hum," I hummed to myself as I started grabbing ingredients for protein shakes.

Gazes narrowing at one another, we exchanged suspicious stares. Almost at the same time, we broke into grins. I shrugged. "At least this way they'll be hot when we get there."

After finishing making our protein shakes, I set one in front of him and grabbed the baking sheets out of the cupboard.

"We only have an hour so they'll have to be soft ginger cookies with no icing, but the man would eat cardboard, so he'll love them," Vidar said as he took the glass container filled with flour from me.

A corner of my lip drew up as I grabbed chocolate chips from the pantry. When we'd been kids Fritz would lick the cheese and sauce from the pizza box. Among his brothers it had earned him the reputation of eating cardboard, though he never actually ate it. In his defense, Pall's Pizza was fit for the Gods.

Vidar's eyes lit up when I put the chocolate chips on the counter. "Great idea! That will make them perfect."

I cut the bag open with a talon and popped one in my mouth. "Chocolate makes almost everything perfect."

Those beautiful, full lips of his quirked up and he bent his six-and-a-half-foot frame down to my level. "You and chocolate," he said with a shake of his head.

Retracting my talons, I brushed his cheek, its gorgeous skin so close to the perfect hue of dark chocolate. "It is my favorite flavor," I said, voice raspy with desire.

Emitting a growl, he pulled me into his arms and pressed his lips to mine. The feel of his hard body against mine, eager, ready, drew a gasp from me. As my lips parted, his tongue entered my mouth. I indulged in his attention for several moments before my anxiety reared back up. He felt it, like he always did, and broke the kiss.

Brushing my nose with his, he hummed. "Yum, chocolatey kisses are the best."

I smiled. "*Your* kisses are the best."

"And they are all yours. You're welcome to more of them, you know," he said, tone suggestive.

Hands on his hips, I pushed him back. "Later, definitely. Right now, we have to replace the cookies you ate before we have to leave to meet your brother."

He held his flour-covered hands up. "It wasn't me, I swear to Frigg!"

Gaze narrowing on his hands, I pointed a talon at him. "You just got flour all over my ass, didn't you?"

Laughter rolled from him. "Maybe."

Grumbling, I brushed flour from my pants. "Get to baking."

He wiggled his dark brows at me. "Can we make out while the batch cooks?"

"Only if you wash those hands."

His grin widened. "Deal."

Pouring the butter mixture into a bowl with the flour, he began stirring with werewolf speed.

After driving twenty-five miles northeast on snowy roads cleared once with a homemade bumper plow, we made it to our meeting point. It was a small parking lot that held fifteen vehicles at most. Only one occupied it now—a dark blue Jeep on massive tires. Fritz's Jeep. A short walk up a hill stood the snowcat, engine rumbling softly like a purr.

The sight of it made my chest tighten. I hadn't spent any time near Fritz since before Vidar had left for college over five years ago now. Back then he'd been a funny, jovial guy who listened to a lot of Bob Marley and wanted peace on Earth. Now, he was a member of the Hemlock Hollow police department. I wasn't sure, but I had a feeling being a cop had changed his sunny demeanor.

I had nothing to fear from HHPD. Among our kind a different set of laws applied to us, and even though it involved killing, my 'profession' didn't break those.

The question was, did I have anything to fear from Fritz Balderson? He was much more than a cop. He was an older brother of the man I loved. If he didn't approve of me, things could get uncomfortable—to say the least.

Vidar put his hand over mine where it clenched the tin that held the cookies so tight it was dimpling it. My gaze focused on the dark skin of his hand.

"I know I've said it a million times, but maybe this time it will sink in. You have nothing to fear. You don't have to impress him," his rich voice filled the cab of the Jeep.

Lifting my gaze, I looked him in the eyes. "He's your brother. He's a big part of your life. You love him," I said.

"Yes."

"And if he doesn't approve of me, it will make things tense between you and I don't want that. You have a wonderful family. I won't take that from you," I said with more fierceness than I intended to let slip.

Holding my gaze, he pried my hand off the cookie tin and cradled it. "You are a part of it, Ayra, a part of me. My family would never treat you as anything less than that." Warm, soothing energy poured from him into me as he smiled gently. "But I understand why you have that fear. The people who brought you into this world and raised you were the monsters, not you. A real family, the one you get to choose now, is different."

My throat tightened too much for me to reply, so I leaned over and kissed him instead. Knowing Fritz was waiting just up the trail, we kept it short.

Cold air swirled around me as I stepped out of the Jeep. I set the cookies aside long enough to put my ski jacket on and zip it up. Though we were extremely resistant to the cold as varúlfur, on the rare chance we came across any humans, it would look extremely odd if we weren't wearing at least some gear. I only wore the shell of my jacket, not the insulated fleece layer that went under it. And beneath that a thin performance wool T-shirt was all I needed.

We grabbed our gear out of the back—skis for me and a snowboard for Vidar—and headed up the trail to the cat. The bright yellow vehicle wasn't massive where snowcats were concerned. It seated four comfortably, five if they wanted to squeeze, and had an area behind the back seats for gear.

Many days of my childhood had been spent in this cat riding into the back country to go skiing off the beaten path. It belonged to Vidar's aunt on his mom's side. He and his brothers had free use of it from the moment they could drive.

The driver door opened, and a tall, dark-skinned man hopped out. Dozens of shoulder length braids poked out from beneath a dark blue beanie with the HHPD shield on it. Sunglasses hid his eyes. He wore a light-weight black and blue jacket, black ski pants, and snowboard boots.

Arms spreading wide, he graced us with a smile so bright white it could power an electric vehicle. "You guys made it! I was starting to wonder."

Tin of cookies held high in one hand, I pointed at Vidar with the other. "He ate all the cookies. We had to make more."

Grunting, Vidar adjusted the bag over his shoulder that held his gear. "Did not," he insisted.

Ignoring him, I handed Fritz the tin of cookies. His grin widened as he accepted them and took the lid off. Drawing in a deep breath through his nose, he closed his eyes. "Ginger cookies with chocolate chips, and they're still warm, perfection!"

He cradled the tin in one arm and opened the back door of the cat with the other. Warmth trickled out, bringing with it the scent of hot cocoa. And not just any hot cocoa, but Balderson hot cocoa. Their mom made the most amazing cocoa. It was pure cocoa powder and cinnamon she ground herself. When we were kids Vidar and I had put away gallons of the stuff while sitting in his room reading comic books. Because of that it was one of my favorite things in the world.

An excited hum came from me as I followed my nose into the vehicle. "Is that your mom's hot cocoa?" I asked.

Vidar climbed in after me and Fritz got in the driver's door. "Mom's recipe, but I made it," Fritz said.

"The perfect thing to go with these cookies," Vidar said.

Lips quirked up to show his fangs, Fritz shot a look over his shoulder at his brother. "You ate all the cookies so she had to make more, and now you want these? Nu-uh, little bro."

"It wasn't me," Vidar insisted as he picked up the tumbler of cocoa in the console on his side.

Smiling, I grabbed the tumbler on my side and basked in the delicious scented steam that wafted from it when I opened the lid.

The engine of the cat hummed as Fritz started up the hill. It climbed the snow with ease, the big tracks holding it atop the deep powder. He wove through the trees with expertise, knowing the backcountry route by heart. It grew steeper and steeper and the cat climbed without noticing it.

"Yum! Ayra, these are delicious!" Fritz said around a bite of cookie.

"Thanks. So's this hot cocoa."

Vidar lifted his chin. "Hey, I helped, a lot."

"Out of guilt for eating the first batch," Fritz threw back with a laugh.

They teased and heckled each other until we were all three laughing. The genuine smile Fritz gave me in the rearview mirror stripped away the years and the wall I'd imagined between us. He asked if we'd seen the latest comic book-turned-movie which sparked a lively conversation because of course we had. Vidar and I were both huge fans of comic books, especially the darker ones.

By the time we reached the top of the mountain I felt like a kid again hanging out with my best friend and his older brother. Fritz had a way of putting those around him at ease. And he talked to me like I was a person instead of a Gods-chosen reaper. It was so refreshing that a weight lifted from my chest.

A bright blue sky fanned out above the snowy mountain peaks. It promised a trip down the mountain with good visibility, which always made for an amazing day skiing. But that wasn't what had me feeling light as the newly fallen snow. It was the smile Fritz gave me when he offered me his hand to help me out of the vehicle. I smirked and accepted it.

That hand meant so much more than help out of a tall vehicle. As a varúlfur, I could fall over a hundred feet without getting so much as a shin splint. As the uppskera, infinitely farther. The hand meant he saw me as the woman, not the werewolf, or even the reaper. And he was offering me his respect and trust.

"Thank you," I said as I excepted his hand.

Smiling so big it gave him dimples, he winked. "Anytime, hvítur úlfur."

White wolf. His childhood nickname for me. It made my chest tighten which surprised me since emotions didn't usually dig their claws into me. Gaze narrowed, Vidar held his hand out to him. Fritz scoffed, laughed, and turned away. Grumbling good-naturedly, Vidar climbed down while Fritz went around and grabbed our gear through the back door.

Leaning against the tracks of the cat, we changed into our ski and snowboard boots. The view replenished my soul. Mountain peaks stretched across the horizon, some so sharp snow couldn't cling to their steep peaks. Between us and them hills of white rolled down through white trees.

Seeing the line I wanted to take had me bouncing in my boots, my heart picking up rhythm in anticipation of the joy of floating down the snow. Little could compare to the free feeling that came with skiing. One of the things that could smiled at me as he set his snowboard over his shoulder. I did the same with my skis and we began hiking after Fritz up the final dozen yards to the edge of the hill.

Fritz pointed to the left. "Be careful of that side. I tested it earlier and it's in danger of sloughing. Don't cut across it, stick to the trees when you can, and you'll be golden," he said.

"Got it. Thanks, bro," Vidar said as they fist-bumped.

Fritz shot me a wink then opened the driver's door. "See you two at the bottom," he said.

Watching the cat turn and go back down the hill, I let out a long breath and my shoulders lowered as the tension went out of me. That went far better than I'd thought it would.

I dropped my skis, knocked the snow from the bottom of my boots off on the bindings, then clicked in. I didn't have poles. I didn't like using them. They threw off my balance. And I felt freer without them.

Beside me, Vidar worked at getting his boots secured in his snowboard bindings. He grinned up at me as he tightened them down. "See, nothing to worry about," he said.

Pulling my goggles down over my eyes, I allowed one corner of my lips to turn up. "You were right."

Eyes popping open wide, he stood up. "I was? I was! Well, of course I was." He pulled his phone out of an inner pocket of his black and green ski jacket. "Could you say that again so I can record it?"

Using my varúlfur speed, I scooped up a handful of snow, squeezed it into a ball, and threw it at him. Raising his arm, he took it on the biceps, laughing. After snapping a selfie of us, he put his phone back in his pocket, placed a green knit cap on his head, then put his goggles on.

"Shall we?" he said through a big, beautiful smile.

The joy in his voice made me smile back. "We shall."

We soared down the mountainside, weaving in and around each other atop the fresh powder. The joy that filled me was made all the sweeter by having Vidar at my side. And it didn't hurt that now I knew his middle brother accepted me for not just what I was, but who I was.

6

HURÐASKELLIR

The slam of a door made me bolt upright in bed. Beside me, Vidar groaned and turned over. Maybe I was hearing things, or maybe the sound had come from my dream. I had been dreaming about a door, one I could escape through to somewhere secluded.

The day of the Wild Hunt had arrived. Dread filled me, and not because of the imagined door slamming. While Vidar's brother had been kind, I didn't dare let myself believe his parents would be as easily won over. Just being with me put their son in mortal peril. How could they not resent me for that?

The worst part was, I didn't even have until tonight to steel myself mentally. Vidar's mother, Leticia, had invited me out for the day.

Staring out the picture window of our loft bedroom at the silhouettes of trees against a brightening blue sky usually brought me serenity. But not today. Sleep had evaded me all night. Still, with the rising of the sun, I was wide awake. Just in case that door slamming wasn't in my dream, I needed to check on it. Leaving Vidar sleeping soundly, I crawled from bed.

I crept downstairs, touching the cedar boughs that decorated the log railing. Their scent wafted up and around me. It comforted me and made me smile as I remembered gathering the fallen branches with Vidar. He loved Yule and had insisted we decorate our cabin with lights, boughs, and decorations. It was impossible to argue when it made him smile so big.

Each day he seemed to find some other area we needed to decorate. He insisted we were forgetting something but considering how the entire place glittered with Yule accoutrements, I couldn't imagine he'd forgotten anything.

A potent smell tickled my nose. Burned cedar branches—Vidar's chosen method of smudging. Had he been smudging downstairs then come back up and fell back asleep? It smelled that way.

A cold breeze drifted around my legs. Following it led me to the door into the garage, which was gaping open. I took a deep breath in through my nose. The scent of latex and cleaner led into the garage. I peered carefully around the open door. Bright daylight spilled into the garage from the ajar door leading out to the backyard. It swayed slightly in a gentle breeze.

Odd, I didn't remember leaving it open. I tiptoed barefoot across the cold concrete floor and closed and locked the door. Vidar must have left it open when he'd been out here. Our kind overheated easily and he enjoyed the fresh air coming in to banish the overwhelming scents of a garage.

I went back inside. Grinning to myself as I thought of Vidar working in the garage, I started making breakfast. Soon the scents of eggs and bacon filled the kitchen. As I was placing steaming plates on the butcher block bar, Vidar came down the stairs, one hand held over a wide yawn.

In only black sweatpants and his panther superhero slippers, he looked better than anything I could fry up. His bare torso of dark, beautiful muscles drew my gaze, which then traveled up his arms where tattoos of knotwork animals swirled around his bulging biceps. By the time my gaze made it to his face, dimples had formed in his cheeks thanks to the huge smile his full lips had turned up into. The gold specks in his green eyes sparkled at me.

Damn. I should not have gotten out of bed so early.

The warmth of that amazing body pressed against me as he stepped close and kissed my forehead. "I'm sorry you couldn't sleep," he said as he went to the coffee pot.

I shrugged. "Don't be. You did your best to wear me out."

Laughing deep and deliciously, he went to the cupboard where we kept the glasses. He got down our favorite mugs—mine being one covered in the face of a black cat and his being one with a mashup of superheroes on it. After filling them, he grabbed chocolate almond milk from the fridge and a small glass jar with liquid chocolate flavored stevia in it. He doctored them up the way we liked them, then sat the cat mug in front of me.

Grabbing one of the plates of food, he sat down at the bar. "Thank you for breakfast. It smells amazing."

"You're welcome," I said awkwardly. Though we'd been together for months now, I still wasn't used to all the agenda free kindness and genuine compliments. We'd been a part for years and they had been very hard years for me in too many ways.

He took a bite of over easy eggs, savored it for an amusingly long time, then cocked his head. "Just like yesterday with Fritz, you have nothing to worry about with my mom today, or my family tonight. They love you."

Only after a long sip of my coffee did I respond. "They loved the meek pup I was. I'm not that person anymore and they won't like what I've become."

Metal clinked against ceramic as he put his fork down a bit hard. "That isn't true in so many ways. You were never meek. You were abused, and you kept getting back up every time you were knocked down. They respected you, just as I did." His eyes softened as he took my hand in his.

I looked down at his big, dark fingers encasing mine and let out a shuddering breath. He went on before I could respond. "And you're the same amazing person deep down in your heart. They will see that, just like I do."

Because I didn't have a good response, I leaned over and kissed him light and quick. "You're the amazing one. Eat your breakfast."

After carefully dripping a tiny bit of hot sauce on my eggs, I dug in. Thankfully, between bites, Vidar changed the subject. The mood lightened as we chatted about yesterday's skiing and riding. We relived some epic tree runs and powder caches. He laughed and gestured excitedly, drawing a smile and even a few chuckles from me.

But the levity was short-lived because the hum of tires on gravel meant Leticia was here.

Vidar opened the door and engulfed his mom in an embrace. She giggled like a girl when he lifted her off her feet. The sound was one of pure joy. It made me smile to know he was so loved by his mother.

Still, the scene was one I'd only ever witnessed from the outside in. The home I'd been raised in was one of hushed voices and tiptoeing, not hugs and laughter. So I stood there stiffly, uncertain how to react.

Though I'd spent a lot of time at his house as a kid, it had usually been when his parents weren't home. That way, word was less likely to get back to my parents about where my hideaway was.

Once Vidar put her down, Leticia strode straight over to me and held her hands out, palms up.

Not one for physical contact, I held my breath as I placed my hands in hers. Rather than pull me in for a hug like I feared, she just held my hands and looked me over. Eyes the same striking green and gold as Vidar's regarded me with a scrutiny that made me want to squirm.

Her long, black hair hung over one shoulder in a beautiful, bulging braid. Despite the freezing weather outside, she wore black yoga pants and a gold tank top that hugged her luscious curves. The only sign she was anywhere near middle aged—which for a varúlfur was over two hundred—were the slight crow's feet at the corners of her eyes. The energy emanating from her felt nurturing and protective—things absent in my own mother.

"You look stressed. Has Vidar not been helping enough?" she asked, shooting a narrowed look at her son at the last.

I shook my head. "Oh no, ma'am. He helps out all the time. He's wonderful."

The grin that graced her lovely face filled her energy with joy. "Good. That's my boy. It must be work then. I have just the cure for that." She looked me over again. "You're over dressed for it. Though you look lovely, of course. You'll want clothes you can relax in." She gestured to herself. "Like mine."

I wore beige linen pants and a silk top of a golden hue that Vidar said made me look "ethereal". I just liked the way the color made my white-blond hair look closer to blond than white.

Gently pulling my hands free of hers, I nodded and dashed upstairs.

"And grab a bundle of that wonderful, dried lavender from your garden," she called up after me."

I decided to follow her example literally. I put on a pair of yoga pants, a sports bra, and a pale blue tank top and hurried back downstairs.

Leticia grinned at me as I descended. "Perfect!" Rubbing her hands together, she wiggled her dark brows. "We'd best get going. We have a busy day planned before a busy night."

The way she said it made it sound like whatever she had planned would take the entire day. Dread made my heart sink as if it had turned to granite. I'd expected an hour, maybe two. But this… There was almost zero chance I could spend all day with Vidar's mother and not completely screw it up.

7

Wolf side scratching just beneath my skin thanks to my anxiety, I focused on breathing. It shouldn't be so hard to simply sit in a vehicle with another female varúlfur. But she wasn't just any werewolf. It didn't matter that my power trumped hers greatly.

I cared so much about her opinion that it gave her power over me. Which was why I kept finding my leg shaking, or my nails tapping on my knee. Despite my mindful breathing, my anxiety rose more the further we drove from the cabin. When Leticia turned her SUV onto the main road, I could hear my heart pounding in my ears.

I flinched internally when she reached over and turned down the music. Without the bluesy voice of Kaleo—an Icelandic band I enjoyed when I wasn't listening to metal—filling the vehicle, the silence was stunning.

"You love my son," Leticia said, the words a statement, not a question.

"With my entire soul, ma'am," I answered without hesitation. "I know that puts him in danger and I—"

She held her hand up and I immediately stopped talking. "Of course it does. But being in love by its very nature puts people in danger. Yet"—she held her finger up again— "to not love is to not live, and I would never wish that on my son."

The words stunned my mind into a numbness that prevented me from responding. Thankfully, it also made my leg stop bouncing up and down. There had to be a 'but' coming.

"You will do everything in your considerable power to protect him." Another statement, as if she knew this for the fact it was.

"Yes ma'am. I would give my life to protect him above all others," I confirmed.

She made an affirmative noise and nodded.

Breath held, I waited for her to go on, but she didn't. The sound of the tires on the snow-covered road filled the vehicle. Then I heard the thudding of my heart and hers. Both were a little elevated. I swallowed and it sounded deafening.

I went back to concentrating on my breathing. In through the nose. Hold. Out through the mouth—as quietly as I could. It helped me maintain calm.

The vehicle began to slow, and Leticia took a left turn onto a side road that cut off into a forest of snowy trees. It led in the general direction of neutral land—land shared by all three packs of Hemlock Hollow. Only one lane had been plowed, and new snow had already begun to start filling it in. Leticia's lifted SUV made easy work of the snow, sitting well above the depth.

Curiosity soon took the place of anxiety. I hadn't been out this way in years. When we were kids Vidar and I had run out here as wolves, exploring the forest and chasing small game. But the area was well over three hundred acres, and we hadn't gone very deep into it.

The road forked. To the left it wasn't plowed and was smooth and clearly untraveled. A single lane was plowed on the right fork. Leticia took the right. Tall pine and fir trees, boughs heavy with snow, lined the narrow road.

"You work so hard for our kind, doing Odin's work, that I want to give something back to you," she said.

Eyes pinching shut tight, I sighed. Not her too. "Please, don't feel that way. I'm not better than any other varúlfur and I don't need or deserve special treatment."

She shook her head. "You misunderstand. I don't want to do it for the uppskera, but the woman, for that little girl who sat in my son's bedroom and read comic books with him, who chased storms with him and danced in the rain in our backyard."

The words, along with the empathy in her eyes made my throat tighten to the point I couldn't swallow. I smiled in answer and looked down at my lap so my hair fell across my face. The burn of tears had become a foreign feeling to me. I'd forgotten how much it stung.

Moments later the SUV eased to a stop. I looked up to find we'd stopped at a large wrought iron gate. Each side of the gate was made up of intricate knotwork that formed the image of a woman with long hair. The gates eased open, each stopping just before the trunk of massive cedar trees that looked as if their tops may brush the clouds. After them the trees thinned, revealing a building.

But this wasn't just any building. It was a long house. It looked to be around twenty-five feet wide and fifty feet long, with a high A-frame style peak. The walls were traditional log, but the roof was a copper-hued metal. Double doors reflected the knotwork woman on the gate, only carved in wood. Runes and falcons had been carved around the door and along the logs that made up the peak.

"Wow, what is this place?" I asked, voice hushed.

Leticia smiled. "This is a temple of Frigg. While tonight is Odin's night with the Wild Hunt, today is Frigg's day." She gave me a somewhat shy look. "I thought you might enjoy celebrating her—and through her, all women—with me today."

Yet again, she managed to choke me up. For someone who got choked up over absolutely nothing, ever, I was having quite a day of it. But then, I'd never had a mother figure treat me with anything other than contempt, disgust, or calculation as to how she could use me to further her agenda. I'd heard of mothers and daughters celebrating Frigg on this day, but my own mother had never done so with me. She had worried that if she coddled me—as she put it—I would get weaker than my thin, frail body already was.

I fiercely shoved thoughts of that horrible woman aside. I wouldn't let her ruin this day for me. "I would be honored," I said.

Joy pulsed from Leticia's power, making her all but glow. Was that moisture in her eyes? I couldn't be sure because she turned her head as she pulled into a spot near the front of the temple.

The real question was, since I was the chosen of Odin and Sonya was the chosen of Frigg, would the Goddess even welcome me in her temple? I kept that fear to myself, though.

"Have you ever been to a sound bath?" Leticia asked.

"No."

Hel, I was new to yoga, having only started doing it since Sonya introduced me to it. As my therapist, she felt it would do me good, bring me peace and balance. And she was right. Of course. She was always right.

149

Laticia beamed, her entire energy lighting up with her smile. "Then you're in for a very special treat, and I'm honored to be the one to take you to your first one."

"What is it? What do I need to do?"

"It's a deep meditation during which a hljóð völva sings and heals your soul through her magic. You don't need to do anything other than relax and breath."

Hljóð völva, a sound witch. I'd heard of them, but I'd never been to one.

The vehicle crunched to a stop on a layer of icy snow. We climbed out into the chilly, bright morning. During our drive the snow clouds had receded, leaving the sun shining in a brilliant blue sky. The temperature was still well below freezing, but the sun made it feel a little warmer.

Leticia led the way up the shoveled path to the temple doors. It was even more beautiful up close, revealing details in the carvings I hadn't noticed from the vehicle. Figures of children played among the knotwork surrounding the doors. Stars and planets were dotted throughout Frigg's long hair.

Before we reached them, the door on the right swung inward. A tall woman with wavy blond and brown hair draping over her shoulders and hanging nearly to her waist stood there. She wore a simple white dress that moved over her curves with the ease of silk. The Othala rune was drawn on her forehead in black.

This was Danía, a member of the Reinhard pack. I knew of her, but I didn't know her. She was a recluse who lived out in the forest and rarely came into town. Part of that was because she was a sort of völva, a witch, who liked the privacy of nature because it helped her connect to the Gods better. Or so I'd heard.

She opened the door wide and beckoned inside with a sweep of her arm. "Leticia, Ayra, welcome to Frigg's temple."

The ground beneath my feet hummed, the sensation increasing with each step closer we got. It wasn't just the ground either. The building itself pulsed. It was neither friendly nor unfriendly. It was simply power, and a lot of it. I hesitated at the threshold, wondering how bad it would hurt to be smite by a Goddess.

A deep breath steeled me with courage—or maybe it was stupidity—and I stepped over the threshold.

8

The moment my foot set down, the power I'd been feeling in the ground and building pulsed through me. My wolf side stirred but didn't rise. The power washed over and through me, cleaning out residual energy from the condemned I'd fought. It left me feeling lighter and energized. Even more amazing than that, it made me feel a profound sense of welcome and belonging.

The beauty of the temple made my breath catch. It was simple, with open wooden beams rising to the high peak and log walls. But it was in that simplicity that the beauty lay. The hardwood floor was open, without the clutter of furniture or trappings, save for one thing. In the center of the room a massive wooden carving of Frigg rose over ten feet tall. The Goddess wore a simple dress, her long hair surrounding her like a cloak. In one hand she held a distaff, in the other she cradled a babe. Stars and planets peaked out through the locks of her hair.

Offerings of holly and evergreen boughs circled the base of the statue. Quartz, amethyst, and different colors of citrine crystals shone among the pine and cedar needles. Somewhere on the other side of the statue a fire crackled, its warmth and scent filling the temple.

Leticia went straight to the statue and lay a small carving at its feet. Now I understood why she'd asked me to bring the dried lavender from my garden. Once she stepped back, I removed it from the canvas bag Vidar had given me to carry it. I closed my eyes.

With the intake of my next breath, I filled my heart with the gratitude I felt for the Goddess.

Thank you, Frigg, for welcoming me into your temple. And thank you for bringing Vidar and his family into my life. Thank you for bringing Sonya into my life. You have blessed me more than I can ever repay you for.

I set the lavender at her feet.

Warmth radiated from the statue, up, and around me. Maybe it was from the fire somewhere on the other side of the room. But something deep inside insisted it was something else.

Smiling at both Leticia and me, Danía beckoned for us to follow and walked around the statue. We followed. Taking up the entire wall at the other end of the temple, was a massive fireplace with a surround formed of river rock. It was big enough for a child to walk in. Within it, yellow and orange flames crackled as they ate at the wood within. A black, metal fireplace screen with the Norse wheel on it held in the embers.

Three plush yoga mats were spread out between the statue and the fireplace. Blankets and bolsters were set up near each one. The middle one had a round mat beneath the rectangular one. On this round mat sat a hand drum, a rain stick, and a copper sound bowl.

Danía dipped her head toward the mats. "Please, choose a mat and get as comfortable as possible so you can slip into a deep meditation. Use the props any way you like."

Without a word to each other, Leticia walked toward the far left one and I went for the far right one. Meditation had become a staple of my self-care, a term I hadn't believed in before meeting Sonya and dating Vidar. So, I knew how I liked my mat setup. I sat in the middle, put the bolster behind my knees, laid down, and folded the blanket under my head.

"Know that this is a safe place, a place protected by the Goddess where none who wish ill-will can enter. Allow your eyes to drift closed," Danía instructed.

It wasn't easy. Closing my eyes meant dropping my guard, trusting the company of those I was with. Trust came hard for me. But I felt the truth of her words. Energy pulsed all around me; in the ground beneath me, the air around me. And it wasn't just Danía and Leticia's power. It was something far greater than any of us in this room, greater even than my uppskera power.

And it felt…protective.

My eyes eased closed.

She then led us through some deep breathing. She had a soothing, melodic voice that eased me into meditation.

"Set your intention for today's practice. It will help your focus return should your mind wander to mundane things like what to cook for dinner or if you need to go grocery shopping," she said.

Leticia laughed softly from the other side of Danía. It was such a lovely, easy sound that it made me smile. My own mother never laughed like that. Hers was more of a cackle.

"I offer some suggestions; the Laguz rune for feminine strength, the Othala rune for heritage, or the Gabo rune for relationships. If none of those call to you, feel free to choose your own. This is your sound bath, your healing," Danía continued. Her voice had begun to take on a rhythm.

Though my mind zinged on Othala, my heart told me the right focus would be Gabo, for relationships. I was here because of my relationship with Vidar, and because I wanted to build one with Leticia. As I thought its name, I pictured the rune in my mind; a large X.

Danía talked us through relaxing our bodies, starting at the crown of our head, moving to our face, shoulders, then down all the way to our toes. She had a wonderful, rhythmic voice that made it easy to let go of tension.

"Honor the Goddess Frigg, honor yourself, and listen to your inner voice," she said.

The ring of a copper bowl filled the room, drowning out the crackling fire for a moment.

"Frigg, All-Mother, Goddess of motherhood, fertility, and knowledge, seer, weaver, and matriarch, we honor you this day," Danía chanted, her powerful voice carrying up into the rafters.

She began to hum, quiet and deep, the sound reaching into my soul and pulling. A drum beat reverberated through the temple, then another, and another. The humming turned into a meandering note that rose and fell. So much power came from that note that it made me shiver. Then she began to sing in time to the drumbeats. When she did, the power coming from her amplified until it felt as though it were lifting me off the ground.

The words were in Icelandic, adding a beautiful flavor to her captivating voice. The song was about Frigg, an ancient one honoring her for her gifts of insight and fertility, honoring her as a woman and a mother. Danía's voice and the drumming pulsed around me, pulling me deeper into the meditation.

Slowly the words and beat fell to the back of my mind. I saw a fjord stretched out before me, tree-covered cliffs rising to frame it. A blue-gray sky reached down to meet the green trees and the dark blue ocean I could see between the cliffs. Pebbles moved under my bare feet and cold water lapped at my toes.

Comforting energy pressed at me from all sides. I felt Vidar's to my left, his brothers', father's, and mother's. To my right I felt Sonya's, Ty's, and many others that I felt like I should know but didn't yet. A profound sense of pack, family, and home filled me.

I looked left and right but found myself standing alone. Their energy was still there with me, though. Something told me this was a place I'd been in another life, and it was a place I'd find myself in again during this life.

The Othala rune pulsed in my mind again. Heritage, home, pack.

I wasn't sure what it meant since I felt as though I had none of those things save for the home I shared with Vidar.

Again I saw the fjord and felt the energy of the others around me. The peace their presence brought reached deep into my heart.

It took a moment for me to realize Danía had stopped singing and the drumming had slowed. Eventually, even the drum stopped. Power still pulsed all around me, but this was the power raised by the music, not the power of those back at the fjord. Still, it was invigorating.

The ring of the bowl sounded again. After it faded, Danía spoke in a soothing tone. "Slowly bring your mind back into your body. Take a deep breath in through your nose and release it slowly through your mouth."

She guided us through two more breaths.

"Begin to awaken your body with small movements, maybe curl your fingers or toes. Extend that to roll your ankles or wrists."

I did as she instructed. My body was slow to respond, lethargic and relaxed in a way I didn't ever remember being. Beneath that relaxation energy buzzed, making my entire body vibrate like it did right before shifting.

"Ease yourself into a seat nice and slow. You might find you're dizzy so there's no rush," Danía instructed.

The woman was prone to understating things. The entire world spun off kilter as I sat up into a cross-legged position. I swayed, having to grab my knees to steady myself.

As she talked us through a few more deep breaths I heard Danía get up and pour something. I opened my eyes as she approached my mat. Smiling, she handed me a green, ceramic mug with a tea diffuser clipped to the rim. Warmth permeated the cup and soaked into my hands.

"This will help ground your soul back in this plane," she said.

"Thank you," I replied, surprised to find my voice didn't come easily.

The alluring scents of apple and spices drifted up from the cup. The smell drew a long sigh from me.

Danía smiled at me. "You're very welcome."

"I saw something during the sound bath," I said.

She nodded. "A vision from Frigg, a personal message just for you."

My instinct was to ask what it meant. But instead I sipped my tea. I knew what it meant. I wasn't alone anymore.

9

As we drank our tea we chatted about sound healing. Danía told us about how she channeled the good will of the Gods as she sang, inviting them in to bring us messages, bless us, or empower us, as was their will.

It fascinated me. The power that had come through her was undeniable. I'd felt it everywhere in the air around me.

As I swirled the last of the tea in the bottom of my cup, I told her, "You have an amazing gift."

A smile lifted her lips. "Thank you. I am lucky to have been so blessed by the Gods," she said with such warmth and sincerity that I knew the comment had touched her deeply.

Sighing, Leticia rose. "We'd best get to gathering boughs. The wreaths won't make themselves," she said with decidedly too much cheer.

All warm and cozy from the fire and tea, I wasn't ready to go traipsing about the forest looking for fallen branches. But I stood too. Leaving the soft mat, I walked to Danía and handed her the cup. "Thank you," I told her with layered meaning.

She nodded and dipped her head. "Thank you."

"Me? What for?"

"For allowing me to get to know the woman behind the uppskera. You should let her out more often," she said.

Heat rose to my cheeks, a rare occurrence for me. Just the feel of it brought the ghost of a smile to my lips. "Thank you for making me feel like I could." I turned to Leticia. "Both of you."

Moisture glimmered in Leticia's eyes. She blinked rapidly, nodded, and looked down as she handed her cup to Danía.

We said our farewells, put our boots and shoes on, and set out into the surrounding forest. Thanks to the snow, there was no path. Walking in human form wasn't easy. But if we shifted, we'd have to leave our clothes behind and walk back naked carrying evergreen boughs. That would test even a varúlfur's ability to stay warm.

So we picked our way carefully through the deep snow. Soon we reached where the forest cast enough shadows to keep a crunchy layer on top. It made for much easier walking.

Several small branches of a massive cedar tree had succumbed to the weight of the snow and broken off. They lay near the trunk, half buried in the burden of white that had broken them. I brushed the snow aside and picked them up. They were beautiful, full boughs, still bright green with their fading life.

"Those are lovely. Great find!" Leticia said.

The compliment made warmth spread through my chest. I handed her one of the boughs. We found a few more on the other side of the tree and gathered those up. Something small beneath one of them caught my eye— an acorn.

I picked it up and rolled it across my palm. "Odd," I said to myself.

"What did you find?" Leticia asked as she leaned close.

Hand extended to her, I let her look. "There are no oak trees around. This is fortuitous. The acorn is a sign of new things to come, strong things that can weather a storm," she said.

A protective feeling for the little thing came over me. I closed my fingers around it.

"Another message from Frigg, perhaps. You should keep it." She nodded to the cedar branches in our hands. "This should do. Shall we head back?"

I nodded, pocketed the acorn, and we started to work our way back to the temple. After long moments of listening to snow crunch under our boots I heard a sniffle.

"Leticia, are you all right?" I asked.

She stopped walking and shook her head. The shine of moisture brightened her eyes as she looked out over the landscape. "You were always such a good girl, so sweet and caring. You fought with bullies twice your size for picking on you and Vidar for reading comic books. You cared for stray cats, for Frigg's sake!"

Unsure of why this would make her cry, I stood there, not knowing what to say.

Another sniffle and she went on. "I knew your parents were cold and focused on elevating their position in the pack, but I never imagined they abused you, and worse, encouraged your brother to do so." The last bit turned into a sob, and she dropped her head into her hands.

Discomfort froze me in place. I wasn't used to people crying. Emotion aside from anger, resentment, and disappointment, had not been shown in my house growing up.

"You couldn't have known. They hid it well," I said softly, not wanting her to hurt for me.

Slowly, she reached out and took my hands. "But I should have. My mother's intuition told me all was not right in your home. I should have listened to it more and acted on it."

Tears ran freely down her dark cheeks, leaving glimmering trails. It hurt me to see them. "You gave me a sanctuary I could come to. You showed me what a loving family looked like. That helped me more than I can ever express."

Sniffling, she opened her arms wide. "May I?"

Against every instinct in my body, I stepped forward into her embrace. It wasn't easy to let people touch me. But when her warm arms wrapped around me something inside softened.

With more sniffles, she soon released me and held me at arm's length. "You are the perfect woman for my son. Never doubt it. I'm not good with words, and I apologize for that. Food is my love language." She laughed at the last part, and I laughed with her.

"Thank you," I said once our laughter subsided.

"You're welcome. Now, shall we go make our wreathes and prepare for tonight?" she asked through a beaming smile.

"We shall," I said with an eagerness that surprised me.

Laughter, smiles, hugs, none of it came easy for me. But somehow this woman made it feel natural and right. She was something special. And now, I was actually looking forward to tonight.

10

That night as Vidar drove us to his parents' house, I was still buzzing from the sound bath. In an odd contrast, I was the most relaxed I'd ever been in my life. The scintillating sound of Vidar's deep voice singing about jingle bells, and the smell of fresh baked ginger cookies filled the vehicle. Baked goods were my contribution to tonight's dinner. Cookies were a specialty of mine, so I felt confident bringing them.

Our intertwined fingers rested on the center console. Snow drifted down onto the windshield, soft enough to require only the occasional sweep of the wipers. The evening was turning out to be as Zen as the day had been. The Wild Hunt could throw the entire thing off kilter, though. We would see. I was feeling oddly…optimistic.

Vidar turned onto the long, twisty driveway that led to his childhood home. His fingers tightened around my hand.

"I'm glad things went so well with you and mom this afternoon. I'm happy you got to relax, have a good time, and bond with her. Tonight is going to be just as amazing, I can feel it," he said.

I clutched his hand back. "I believe you," I said in all honesty. It made him smile, and that made me smile.

This man was slowly burning away the darkness of the last several years I'd spent without him. And things weren't just returning to how they'd been when we were kids. They were infinitely better. It both thrilled and terrified me.

He lifted my hand to his lips and kissed the back of it.

When we pulled up before the Balderson's A-frame cabin, the entire family were sitting out on the covered porch. Holiday lights of varying colors lined the eaves and surrounded the large wooden front door. Those lights combined with the golden glow of a firepit to light up the front porch. Leticia and Balder sat beside the firepit, sipping from mugs. Vidar's brothers Fritz and Rúnar sat at a table playing a game.

Seeing them all didn't strike the same dread into me that it would have yesterday. I got out and grabbed the container of cookies from the backseat before Vidar even made it around to my side of the vehicle. Brows raised, he smiled at me and took my free hand in his. The contentment that radiated from him made me smile in return.

I would give anything to make this man happy, even fit in with people when my instinct was to be a recluse. But the last few days had shown me that these people were different. What I'd seen of them as a child had seemed too good to be true. Time with them was proving that it wasn't.

Careful of the spots of ice, we made our way up the snow-packed walkway to the steps leading up to the porch. The steps were clear thanks to heated pads. We made our way onto the deck. Thanks to being covered, it held a lot of heat from the firepit. The closer we got to his parents, the warmer it grew.

Leticia shrugged the blanket off her shoulders and stood. Setting his mug on the firepit surround, Balder stood as well. Out of uniform the police chief looked far less intimidating. Without a hat on, his dark-skinned, bald head shone varying colors each time the holiday lights changed. His easy smile and warm, brown eyes put me at ease.

"Ayra, we're so happy you came," Balder said.

With his big, happy eyes and out turned palms, he looked very much like he wanted to hug me. Though I returned his smile, I bladed myself to him slightly to discourage any excessive contact.

"Thank you for inviting me, sir."

He held his hands up and shook his head. "There'll be none of that. Call me Balder," he insisted.

Rather than replying, because I knew I'd slip up, I nodded. He'd been telling me that since I was a kid. I hadn't been able to do it yet.

"I smell ginger cookies!" Fritz said as he stepped around his dad.

I extended the container of cookies to him. He accepted them and darted in to plant a quick kiss on my cheek. It took everything in me to remain still and not take him out at the knees on instinct alone. Considering that might possibly be the worst way to start this night, I was infinitely glad I didn't.

He reached around me and playfully punched Vidar in the shoulder. "Hey, little bro."

"Hey, middle bro," Vidar called back with plenty of snark.

Ignoring him, Fritz peeled back the lid of the container and took a long breath in through his nose. He cast a disarming grin my way. "With chocolate chips. You're the best!"

"Again, I helped make them," Vidar said as Fritz walked back to the table where Rúnar sat still staring at their game.

Wooden pieces carved to look like something between a pawn and a soldier spread across a checkered board. Two-thirds of the pieces were stained a brown so dark they were almost black while the other third were a pale wood that were simply clear coated. One white piece was taller than all the other pieces—the king.

After another moment of deep contemplation, Rúnar moved one of the white pieces two spaces.

"You like Hnefetafl, Ayra?" Fritz asked as he sat back down. "You can play me after I kick Rúnar's ass."

"Language, Fritz!" his mom called over in sharp warning.

Fritz flinched. "Sorry, mom."

Expression stoic, Rúnar flicked a pretzel at him, striking his brother in the forehead.

It took more concentration than I liked to keep my heartrate steady and my energy from spiking. In a long-sleeve, button-up, silk shirt of a lovely gold, Rúnar Balderson blended holiday sheik and business casual. In contrast to his dred-rocking middle brother and his superhero loving little brother, he exuded an air of professionalism even while relaxing on his parents' porch during the holiday. Which came as no surprise considering he was an FBI agent.

"I do like Hnefetafl," I said. "But, Rúnar just beat you."

Fritz's eyes popped open wide, and his attention shot to the board. "Ah, man."

Everyone burst into laughter. A chuckle even slipped from me. It was worth it when Rúnar gave me a warm smile. He took one of the cookies from the container Fritz held and dipped his head to me. "Thank you. These smell amazing."

"You're welcome," I said, allowing a little smile to slip through.

"I helped," Vidar grumbled.

"Of course you did, dear," his mom said as she patted him on the cheek.

I loved their interactions with each other, always had. As a kid they'd been like one of those happy sitcoms to me—an example of an amazing, loving family.

Looking out at the full moon hovering over the forest, Balder began to unbutton his flannel. "Shall we hunt?" he asked, voice eager and suddenly deeper.

Energy rose all around me, filling the evening air with eager anticipation. No one responded though. They all looked to me, even Vidar. They were deferring to me not because I was the uppskera, but because I was their guest. My wolf side stirred, and excitement rose within. I'd wanted to run with this family my entire life. To run with other wolves was to move, to be, as a pack.

"Yes," I said.

We all began shedding clothing at once. The chill of the sub-zero air kissed my bare skin for only a moment. Since Leticia and Balder were the heads of the family, we waited for their cue. The moment they'd stripped naked, they looked at one another, then leaped from the deck. Their human bodies poured into those of black wolves by the time their paws touched the snow.

Vidar smiled at me and the sheer power of joy in his expression made me smile back. We leaped after his parents together. I felt his brothers follow. A beat later I was surrounded by black wolves. In contrast, my white paws blended in with the snow beneath them. Discomfort settled over me as they trotted in circles around Vidar and me. But their howls and yips were happy and excited.

The sounds felt…welcoming.

Tails wagging, tongues lolling out, their energy was so warm and welcoming that it made my eyes sting.

The circling ceased. Noses low and tails high, Leticia and Balder took off running for the forest. Yips and barks filled the crisp air as we all ran after them. I may have even let out one of my own. Elation coursed through me with every pump of my heart.

I'd only been on a Wild Hunt with my parents and brother a few times. As a pup I'd been too slow, too weak, to keep up. Those early years were burned into my memory. I'd tried to go with them, only to be left alone and shivering with fear in the forest at night. After a few years, I'd given up and just stayed home. When I grew stronger as a teenager, I didn't want to go any more than they wanted me to. So I never tried again.

Now I was one of the strongest varúlfur alive. I could outrun any wolf. But my confidence and joy didn't come from that. It came from knowing the wolves I was running with now would never leave me behind. In fact, their pace was more of a lope than an all-out run.

Fritz and Rúnar even took the time to swat one another playfully and bite at Vidar's tail. They occasionally chased each other in circles around us.

The scent of rabbit came to me on the air. All play ceased immediately as everyone else smelled it too. Our attention snapped to the elders. As was tradition, the matriarch scented the air, then gave the snout dip of approval. Together, she and Balder took off like twin arrows. The four of us dashed after them. Rúnar and Fritz fanned out to flank their left while Vidar and I fanned out to flank their right.

I kept pace with Vidar, careful not to draw ahead of Leticia or Balder. The adrenalin pumping through my canine body made it difficult. But I would never do anything to disrespect them.

Trees whipped by. Crisp air flowed into my snout, forming ice crystals on my whiskers. The chill was almost as invigorating as the company. New snow drifted down about me, the flakes lazily making their way to the ground. The top layer of snow was frozen just enough that my paws didn't break through it as we ran.

The thrill of the hunt mingled with the excitement of running with wolves I trusted and cared for. It was almost like having a pack—something I never thought I'd experience.

We burst from the trees into a small clearing. I caught sight of a small, white form with long ears. Then Leticia was suddenly upon it. We fanned around her in a circle. She held it beneath a paw, not in her jaws as I'd expected.

Balder lifted his snout skyward and let out a long howl of celebration. Vidar and his brothers joined in. Compelled by their songs, I lifted my snout and released a howl of my own. We sang together for several wonderful moments before returning our attention to Leticia.

Lifting her paw, she revealed the trembling rabbit. She dipped her nose to it. Rather than break its neck like I expected, she nudged it. When it didn't move, she nudged it again. Slowly, the rabbit rose. It flicked its ears back and forth. Then suddenly, it took off running again. Leticia let it go.

My instincts screamed at me to give chase. But no one else did, so I held my ground. Head cocking to the side, I looked at Vidar. He gave me a big, wolfy smile, tongue lolling out one side of his mouth. Leticia and Balder began jogging back toward the house. I could only stare after them.

Such a show of mercy stunned me. It also impressed me.

Vidar licked the side of my face, shocking me from my stupor. I nipped at his ear. He barked, dipped his shoulders down, then hopped up on his hind legs for a moment. Shaking my head, I took off after his parents and brothers. He trotted along beside me, grinning in the disarming way only canines could.

This night was turning out to be nothing like I expected, and I couldn't be happier.

11

ASKASLEIKIR

The night left me exhausted, but in the most wonderful way. After we returned from our hunt, we set hay out in the yard for Sleipnir, Odin's horse, and the steeds of the other involved in the Wild Hunt. It was ceremonial, of course, a symbol of respect to Odin and the honored dead who rode with him this night. After that we feasted, then gathered around a bonfire in the backyard and burned the wreathes we made to honor Balder and encourage the return of the sun in the coming year.

Through it all his parents and brother included me as though I were one of them. It left me reeling in the best possible way. When we pulled into the garage of our cabin I wanted nothing more than to collapse into bed wrapped in Vidar's arms.

"Ice-cream first, then bed?" he said in a hopeful voice I couldn't say no to.

"Of course," I said.

A meow greeted us as we walked into the hallway. I reached down to pet Heimdallr. He purred and head-butted my hand as I did so. As Vidar stopped by the bathroom, I went to the kitchen to get the ice-cream. The scent of burnt cedar hung heavy in the air again. It was too fresh to be hours old, making me wonder if Vidar had gotten a cedar scented candle or something. Most varúlfur didn't like scented things like that due to our sensitive noses, but I was still getting used to living with Vidar. It could be a little quirk of his.

Dodging the cat weaving between my feet, I went to the cupboard the bowls were in and opened it. The spot where they went was empty. I didn't remember us using them all, but maybe Vidar had his best friend Ty or maybe some old high school buddies over while I'd been out with his mom today. I couldn't smell anything over the burnt cedar, so who knew.

I checked the dishwasher. No bowls.

As I felt Vidar's energy approaching, I asked, "V, what did you do with all the bowls?"

"Put them in the cupboard."

I checked the other cupboard in case he had decided to move things around. "Which one?"

The scent of snow and woodsmoke surrounded me as he reached over me and opened the first cupboard I'd checked. "This one. What the…?" He joined me in checking the other cupboards.

"Are you sure?" I prodded.

Giving up, he crossed his arms and gave me a hard look. "One hundred percent." One of his dark brows slid up. "You know what this is."

Groaning, I rolled my eyes and kept searching.

"Candles, skyr, milk, cookies, and now bowls," he continues.

I held up a hand. "Don't say it."

"It's the Yule lads. We haven't decorated boots and put them out. We've offended them."

Ceasing my searching, I dropped my head into my hand.

"The evidence is irrefutable," he insisted.

I threw my hands up in the air. "Okay, okay. I'll go get boots. You get the decorations."

"Woo hoo!" he called out as he darted for the garage. The pure joy in his tone made me regret holding out so long against this decoration.

My brother was dead and still he controlled me from Hel. I had to learn to stop giving him power over me.

The only boots I could think of were a pair of old ski boots. If I took the liners out of them there would be plenty of room to place little treats 'for the Yule lads' inside. I dashed upstairs and dug them out of the closet. They were even red. I pulled the liners out to make more room in the boots.

When I got back downstairs, Vidar had craft items strung all across the bar—bits of evergreen branches, holly, craft paper, glue, ribbons, even glitter.

I pointed to the glitter. "No."

The delight in his eyes made them sparkle as bright as the glitter. Instead of replying, chuckled maniacally.

"Fine. But since we're doing this, I'm making hot cocoa."

"Oooo, with candy canes!"

His child-like enthusiasm made me laugh.

As I started the hot cocoa, he cleaned the boots.

Soon, the scents of chocolate and peppermint filled the air.

"I can't believe you have me decorating boots," I said as I stuffed an oversized canvas stocking inside my boot.

He shook his head. "Not me, the Yule lads."

A disbelieving *humph* came from me.

"You can't believe in the children-eating Jólakötturinn and not the Yule lads!" he said.

I lifted my chin. "I didn't say I didn't believe in them. I just don't believe in rewarding pranksters."

Head cocking to the side, he smiled. "But you'll appease a giant cat who eats people who don't get new clothes for Yule."

"Of course. I don't want to be eaten by a giant cat."

He shrugs. "Naturally."

We chatted, laughed, and drank our hot cocoa as we decorated the boots. Laughter didn't come easy for me, but Vidar had a way of drawing it out. He brought all the best parts of me to the surface, some parts that I'd thought were long gone.

When we were done, we had transformed two old ski boots into something...well, something.

"Should we put them out tonight?" I asked.

"Naw, it's snowing like crazy out there. I'll shovel the deck in the morning, then we can put them out."

I regarded the monstrosity before me with doubt. "Mine looks like the holiday section of a craft store threw up on it."

Vidar's, on the other hand, looked amazing. Of course. He'd found faux fur and cut and glued it around the top of the boot, painted white stripes all along the plastic shell of the boot to make it look like a candy cane, and put white, fluffy balls down the front.

He put an arm around me as he looked at my glitter bombed mess. "Van Gogh is just a different type of artist than Michael Angelo."

Lips pursed and eyes pinched into a glare, I turned to look at him. "I'm not sure if that's a compliment or insult."

He chuckled, then kissed the top of my head.

"Oh now I *know* it's an insult!" I said with a laugh as I struck him in the abs.

His chuckle erupted into full-blown laughter and he began to tickle me. With a squeal, I leaped off the barstool and ran around the bar. He gave chase.

"You can't escape Superwolf!" he called out as I dashed for the living room.

Laughter eventually got the better of me and he snagged me in mid-leap over the ottoman. He attempted to throw me down on the couch but I twisted us so I ended up on top. My long, white-blond hair spilled down around me, brushing his chest. The heat and intensity in his green eyes made muscles between my legs tighten.

I started to lean down for a kiss, but he spoke and his words froze me in place. "Be my mate."

He couldn't possibly mean...

One corner of my mouth turning up, I said, "We mate all the time."

Instead of reply, he gave me a serious look that raised bumps along my arms. I crawled off him and sat near his feet. "But V. I..."

Sitting up, he grabbed both my hands in his. "May not have time or the ability to give us children, may have to hunt down condemned for the rest of our lives, may die fighting those condemned. I know, I know all these things. And they don't alter my desire to be your mate one single bit."

"But you deserve those things," I said without looking up.

He pulled my hands in to his chest. "I deserve to have what I want. And the only thing I want in all the nine worlds, the only thing I'll ever want in all the nine worlds, is you," he said, voice low and deep with feeling.

Words wouldn't come to me. The hint of a smile made a dimple form in his left cheek. "If it's too soon, I'll wait. If that isn't what you want, I'm happy as we are. But know that I am all in forever."

Recalling the lesson from Danía yesterday, I listened to my inner voice.

"I'll be your mate," I said. I already belonged to him heart, body, and soul, so why not?

Eyes widening, he sat up straighter. "Really?"

"Really."

Letting out a joy-filled whoop, he swept me up, rose, and spun me around. Somehow, he managed not to knock either of us into the coffee table. The moment he stopped spinning us, I wrapped my legs around him and kissed him.

His lips parted for me instantly. The flavors of chocolate and peppermint burst anew across my tongue. I breathed deep through my nose, drawing in his woodsy scent. I wanted to draw every part of him into me, particularly the hard part pressed against my pelvis. But when my hands began to explore him, he broke the kiss and put me down.

Hands on my shoulders, he took a step back. His power pulled at mine. Though he panted with desire, he shook his head. "We have to cleanse tonight, or we won't get Freyja and Freyr's blessing."

The mating ceremony was preceded by a night of cleansing in which the couple underwent ceremonial bathes and abstained from sex until the ritual the following night. Unlike marriages that could have long engagements, once a couple agreed to the mating ceremony, it always happened the following night. It wasn't a big event with friends and family attending. It was private, just between the couple and the Gods.

I groaned. "A silly tradition."

"You said that about setting out boots for the Yule lads, and look where that got us," he countered.

"Fine." I leaned in close so he'd feel my breath on his neck. "But when I'm in the bath touching myself, I'll imagine it's your hands. And when my fingers are inside me, I'll be imaging your cock."

A full body shudder rocked him, and he groaned. "That is so unfair," he said as he let out a long breath.

Moving away from him, I gave him a crooked smile. "You know I don't play fair."

I put a little extra sway in my hips as I started for the stairs. "I'm *really* dirty. Guess I'd better go run that bath."

The sling of curses in Icelandic that drifted up after me made me smile. They were deliciously filthy. While I was in the bath, they would give me all kinds of inspiration.

12

After a nearly sleepless night and an afternoon of preparing, I should have been exhausted. Instead, I was keyed up to the point I couldn't sit still. After breakfast I'd trimmed my pubic hair, toenails, fingernails, shaved my legs, meditated and prayed to Freyja and Frigg, and even did a yoga flow dedicated to cleansing my energy. Once I was done I cleaned all fifteen hundred square feet of our cabin.

While I'd been busy doing all that, Vidar had been somewhere out on our property preparing the place our ceremony would occur. He'd left shortly after dawn.

Since the day required a fast, I hadn't even had breakfast or lunch to distract me or take up my time. Water was the only thing I'd ingested, which also meant I was starving.

Finally, as evening approached, I stripped naked and went out onto the back deck. We kept it shoveled so no snow was on it, but there was an icy layer that melted beneath my warm feet. At twenty or so degrees out, even as a varúlfur it was cold enough out to harden my nipples and give me chill bumps. My body adjusted quickly. In only a breath the chill was gone, and I was comfortable. Not even the breeze coming across our snow-covered back yard that lifted my long hair felt cold.

Our backyard was more of a field that stretched for over sixty feet before leading into and evergreen forest. The sun barely hung over the tops of the trees, already setting the mountains it touched aglow with pinks and purples. Vidar's energy approached from within that forest. It tugged at my own power, but I held my ground.

A big, black wolf stepped from the long shadows of the forest reaching across the snowfield. Tilting his head up to the cloudy sky, he let out a long howl. It plucked my energy like the string of an instrument. I felt it all the way down to my core.

Once he reached the backyard, I leaped from the second story deck. As I fell through the air, I transformed from woman to wolf. My white paws met the packed snow. Mouth gaping and tongue lolling, he began to circle me. Those stunning green and gold eyes of his held me with a magnetic force. The eagerness within them reflected my own.

The left corner of his mouth lifted into a very human half-smile. At the sight, I took off like a bolt thrown from Odin's staff. I ran at full speed until I reached where Vidar's paw prints disappeared into the trees. Dodging low hanging branches and tree wells created by snowfall made for slower going. But that wasn't the only reason I slowed.

I wanted plenty of energy for what came after.

At my flank, Vidar began to push me to the right. I dashed that direction and picked up speed again. We ran and danced, flowing through the forest and around each other. He was my match in speed and agility—so long as I didn't use my uppskera power, which of course I wouldn't. He herded me the direction he wanted and I didn't fight it.

Having him chase me was exhilarating in a way I hadn't expected. It brought up raw, primal need and desire. Part of me wanted to let him catch me now, but I knew we weren't to wherever he was directing me yet. So we ran through the forest, giving ourselves over to the joy of it.

Darkness was quickly laying its claim on the land. By the time we broke free of the forest, the clouds on the horizon were orange as fire. The sun had fallen beneath the mountains, outlining their snowy silhouettes in gold. Near the base of a hillside at the edge of the trees, steam rose from the snow. The scents of minerals and freshly cut pine drifted on the air.

It was there that Vidar drove me.

As we grew closer, I realized the steam was rising off a turquoise hued pool of water. Heat radiated from it. Behind it stood a finely crafted lean-to of fresh logs with a roof of cedar boughs. Runes had been carved into the bark of the supporting logs; Gabo for gift and relationships, and sex, Elhaz for protection and defense, and Ehwaz for loyalty, partnership, and trust. Beneath the lean-to, blankets lay atop an inflatable camping mattress. Between the pool and the lean-to stood a small ring of stones with wood piled in their center.

I stopped before the pool and turned to face Vidar. When he drew close, we circled one another in a slow trot. He nipped playfully at my white tail. My right front foot broke through the surface of the snow. I went with it, going down onto my stomach, then rolling over onto my back. He was on me in an instant.

Front legs to either side of my shoulders and rear straddling my hips, he hovered over me. At nearly the same time, we both transformed into humans. Due to the heat the process generated, the snow beneath me melted, hardening into ice almost immediately.

Our chests heaved so much they touched, not from exertion, but from excitement. When his pectorals brushed my hard nipples I let out a little groan. I wanted him to lower his body onto mine and sink deep into me. But with his powerful thighs to either side of mine, I couldn't spread my legs.

I had the power to do it forcibly. But there were other things we had to do before we could indulge in each other.

Bending his head down, Vidar bit me on the neck, not hard enough to hurt, but almost. The feeling and meaning sent a thrill shooting straight to my core. I gasped and lifted my hips out of instinct. His very hard cock brushed the shorn hair over my pubic bone. Another groan pulled from me.

Breath heaving in and out with need, Vidar released my neck. Suddenly, the warmth of his body hovering over mine was gone. His dark-skinned hand came back into my field of vision. I accepted it and let him help me to my feet. The skin of my back peeled from the ice audibly.

Still holding tight to my hand, he led me to a boulder near the hot spring pool. At three feet tall and two feet around, the stone was massive. The top of it was semi-flat. Due to the way it sat on the snow, it was clear he had carried it here. It had to weigh hundreds of pounds, but that was little for a varúlfur of his strength.

An altar, handpicked and created by him for us. It touched something deep inside me.

Next to it sat a bundle of lavender, holly with bright red berries, sprigs of evergreen, a canteen, and a small burlap pouch. Vidar dipped his head to me, then let go of my hand and let me approach the altar first.

I took a few deep, cleansing breaths as I walked up to it. Taking up the lavender and holly, I knelt in the snow before the stone.

"Freyja, I honor you on this, the night of my mating. If it pleases you, I ask that you bless our joining in all ways you see fit," I said as I placed the lavender and holly on the altar.

The holly gave me a chill and more than a little anxiety. It represented fertility. I'd never seen myself as having children, not even when I was younger, and my family life hadn't been quite as dark. But with Vidar, all things were possible. Much to my shock, that didn't scare me as much as I thought it would.

I rose and moved aside so he could approach. He gave me a surprisingly shy smile as he passed me. Taking up the evergreen sprig, he knelt in the divot my knees had left in the snow.

Eyes closing, head tilting back, he spoke. "Freyr, I honor you on this, the night of my mating. If it pleases you, I ask that you bless our joining in all ways you see fit." With that, he placed the evergreen next to the holly and lavender.

He picked up the small bag and reached toward me. Hands clasped, we rose together. We walked out into the snowy field. The path had been beaten down by hum earlier in the day, so thankfully we didn't sink. We stopped close to the base of the hill where he'd cleared the snow in a fifteen-foot-long swath, exposing the ground five feet beneath the snow. The hill was actually just the snow he'd cleared away.

We knelt together on the rock-hard ground at one end of the cleared space. Without a word, we both extended our claws and began to dig. Varúlfur claws were tough as steel, so they cut right through the frozen ground. It took only a few moments for us to dig a hole a foot deep and just as wide in the dirt.

From the bag, Vidar removed peat moss and placed it in the hole. Then he dug out a brown seed. I knew it by both scent and sight—an ash tree seed. He placed it in my hand, then cupped his hand beneath mine. Together we lowered it into the hole, spreading our fingers until it fell into the peat moss.

As one, we said, "Together we plant this seed of Yggdrasil as a symbol of our undying commitment to each other."

After covering the tree with the soil we'd removed, and over a foot of snow, we walked to the other end of the cleared space. We repeated the process there with a second seed.

Without the fur of my wolf form I was aware the air was cold. It wasn't unbearable because my kind's body temperature was natural higher. The cold felt better to me, more easeful than heat. Still, that steam rolling off the hot spring was starting to look enticing.

Ritual complete, Vidar and I rose and faced each other. Though I was aware of his muscular body and very erect cock, my gaze didn't travel over any of it. I couldn't look away from his eyes. The kindness, gentleness, and profound love that radiated out from their green and gold depths stirred a fire in me as hot as Midgard's core.

One step closed the distance between us. His hands cupped my ass and lifted me effortlessly. I wrapped my legs around his waist and my arms around his neck. The hard planes of his body pressed against both the hard and soft curves of mine. The outline of his cock against my pelvis and lower abs made my core muscles clench.

Our lips met with gentle reverence. As we kissed, I was vaguely aware of him walking, carrying me closer to the warmth of the pool. Water so hot it felt close to scalding touched my toes. In a few moments, my feet warmed, and my body adjusted. Once it did, the water began to rise; up my legs, over my ass, and to my waist. It stopped there and my feet touched stone.

Vidar had walked up into the pool and sat down, all with me still wrapped around him. The man had dexterity and grace in spades. And knowing he was all mine, and would forever be from this moment on, made me hotter and wetter than any hot spring could.

A long sigh slid from my mouth into his as I acclimated to the hot water. The chill of winter still touched my cheeks, but the contrast with the water made it pleasant. The sensations combined with the feel of Vidar's body beneath mine made every nerve in my body sing.

His strong hands moved from caressing my butt to stroking my back. Every touch felt super-charged, like he was feeding energy straight into my skin from his. My wolf stirred, making me realize it didn't just feel like it, he really was feeding me energy.

Afraid my uppskera power of energy stealing was kicking in, I broke the kiss. It had never happened before while we were having sex, but the similar feeling made me worry. The last thing I wanted to do was steal his energy.

Immediately knowing what I was thinking, Vidar shook his head. "It isn't your power. It's the mating."

He held his hand before us, turning it back and forth. It glowed a mixture of lavender and gold. "See. Your energy is flowing into me too," he said.

Fascinated, I reached my hand toward his. The glow leaped between us, flowing from me to him, then back to me. It tingled in an enticing way that shot straight down between my legs. His erection flexed between us, telling me it had the same effect on him.

Pulling my hand away, I watched the energy stretch between us. He chuckled. "That tickles."

I pressed my palm to his and interlaced our fingers. The tingling became a pleasant buzzing. Grinding my pelvis against his erection, I bent to kiss that gorgeous smile. Hands and tongues exploring each other, we gave in to the building desire. He dipped his head into the water and drew one of my nipples into his mouth.

Moaning, I pressed harder against him, gripping the back of his head. I dug my fingers into his short, black curls. He moved to the other breast as I rose onto my knees to get his head out of the water. My core pulsed, longing to be filled by him. Like always, he sensed my need and slid two fingers deep inside me.

"Gods!" I cried out as I threw my head back.

Tongue flicking my nipple, fingers pumping inside me, he groaned.

Water splashed as he picked me up. Smile turning mischievous, he set me on the rock ledge at the edge of the pool and pushed my knees apart. Thanks to the hot spring the rock was ice-free and warm to the touch. The air, however, was not. But as he knelt in the water and pushed my legs apart, my body generated more than enough of its own heat.

He spread the lips of my sex and stared for a long moment. Then he began to kiss, nip, and lick his way up my inner thigh. It took an agonizingly long time for him to reach the apex of my legs. When he did, he took one long, slow lick of my slit, then devoted his attention to my clit. As he rubbed, circled, and flicked it with his tongue, his slid two fingers deep inside me.

Crying out, I collapsed back onto the bank of the pool. He played me like an instrument, drawing little sounds of pleasure out of me with each wonderful movement he made. The pressure of an orgasm built and built until I was gasping from being kept on the precipice.

At last, it broke over me like a meteor shower, sending a million sparks of pleasure shooting through my body to completely rock my world. My core muscles spasmed over and over, clutching his fingers. My body bucked off the ground. Eyes slamming shut, I swore I saw the stars falling behind my lids.

When my body relaxed back onto the ground, I slowly opened my eyes. Vidar stared up at me from between my legs, a crooked grin giving him a devious look. I grinned back. He scooped me up and pulled me back into the water.

Warmth enveloped me. He sat me on a rocky shelf and spread my legs again. The touch of something much bigger than his fingers pressed at my entrance. Despite the water, his energy still tingled upon my skin, concentrating between my legs. Our gazes locked. The intensity in his eyes made my heartbeat kick back into high gear. I raised my hips. The smooth head of his erection slid into me, followed by his iron-hard length. He filled me to the brim, the head touching the end of my channel just as his balls touched my butt cheeks.

The energy that tingled along his skin spread from his erection to my vaginal walls. Intense pleasure erupted through me. It was as though his energy turned my entire channel into a g-spot. We groaned in unison. Then he began to move, and my entire world exploded with pleasure unlike anything I'd ever felt.

We cried out in unison.

He withdrew slowly, then pushed back in. Breathe held, I lifted my hips, angling them so he could seat himself fully inside. Gazes still locked, we moved together in a slow, perfect rhythm.

Lips quirking up, he brushed a lock of wet hair from my cheek. "Breathe, my white wolf," he said. With that he thrust into me fast and hard.

Air left my lungs in a gasp. I dug my nails into his back. "Only for you," I said, voice so breathy it barely sounded like my own.

That opened a flood gate. Rhythm speeding up, we gave ourselves over to the instinct to become one. I came again as he exploded inside me—both literally, and energetically. Vision going white, I clung to him as my body bucked against his. His power shot through every atom of my being from the inside out. I felt mine do the same to him as I clung to him to keep from spinning off the world.

Once the muscle spasms of the most intense orgasm of my life began to abate, I felt something amazing in place of the pleasure. A deep connection that made every part of me buzz strung between us like a steel cord—unbreakable, eternal, weaving us into one.

So this was the mate bond. The stories had failed miserably to describe how amazing it was.

Vidar panted in my ear, his head collapsed onto my shoulder, the bank of the pool hard against my back. But I loved each sensation; the tickle of his breath, the crisp air in contrast to the hot water, the scratch of his five o'clock shadow on my cheek, his body on mine, in me. His energy woven unbreakably to mine. It was perfection.

13

The brightening sky of dawn woke me. No, that wasn't it. The cold spot in the bed where Vidar should have been woke me. The fire he'd lit near the entrance of the lean-to had gone out and the warmth the walls caught had dissipated. It wasn't cold thanks to the battery powered electric throws on the bed—one beneath me and one over me. But even those were cooling as their batteries gave in to the sub-zero air.

Footsteps approaching told me Vidar wasn't far away. I knew it was him, not by the rhythm, but by the feel of his power and the cord between us.

Lifting my arms over head, I stretched long and slow and let the blankets pile into my lap. Cold air teased my skin, but my body adjusted quickly enough.

Outside the lean-to a clear, blue sky met the white mountains. I stared at the pristine, snowy landscape for a long moment. Snow-covered evergreens blanketed the hills that led to sharp-peaked mountains of perfect white.

I swung my feet over the side of the air mattress and reached for the bag that contained the clothes Vidar had brought for us. The man had thought of everything. I wasn't sure why the Gods had brought us together, but I was grateful beyond measure. He stepped around the side of the lean-to and grinned when he saw me.

"Good morning, beautiful," he said.

In black sweatpants and a dark green, long-sleeved T-shirt that set off his eyes, he looked pretty amazing himself.

Forgetting my clothes, I rose and went to him. He enveloped me in a warm embrace. Bending, he kissed me with a tenderness that made me want to sink into him. But my stomach growled, reminding me I had other needs as well.

He drew back with a laugh. "Sounds like we need to get you some food."

One shoulder rising, I blew out a breath. "Unfortunately."

That elicited a laugh from him. He turned me around and slapped me on the ass. "Go, take care of nature's call. I'll pack up."

Laughing, I dashed out to do just that. When I returned he had packed everything, including the air mattress, and placed it all on a travois. Only the lean-to remained. He made an appreciative noise as I strode barefoot across the snow. He gave me a wink, then motioned to my clothes sitting on top of the travois. I grabbed them and quickly dressed.

The short trek back to the cabin was filled with his stories of holidays with his family. They sounded so normal, so wonderful. It was hard to believe that they were my family now. He admitted that he'd told them about his plans to ask me to perform the mate-bond ritual. I was shocked to learn each of them had encouraged him. They wanted me as part of their family. Me, the woman who made their son happy, not the uppskera. To be wanted by a family was a new and amazing feeling.

The cabin hadn't even come into view when I felt the press of energy that meant other shifters were near. Three spots of slight energy pulsed stronger as we grew closer. A breeze blew their scents to me and I knew who it was even before the front porch came into view and revealed them to me.

Three boys, each no older than thirteen, sat on our porch, my old, decorated ski boots between them. Candy wrappers were piled in their laps, along with wrapping paper and ribbons. Chocolate rimmed their mouths. Two were blond and the third, biggest boy, had brown hair, all worn back in long braids.

Hands on my hips, I strode up to them with a carefully faked mask of irritation on my face. "Kris, Jon, and Emil. I should have known you three were the 'Yule lads' terrorizing us!"

Eyes going wide, the boys leaped to their feet.

I spun back to face them. "You three!" I shook my head as I walked to the bottom of the steps. "Admit it, you little sons of Loki, it was you who stole our candles, cookies, skyr, and milk."

Kris, the brown-haired boy, eldest and tallest, nodded. "Yes ma'am. It was us." He shot a side glance at Vidar. Both were struggling not to smile.

I turned to point at my mate. "Or should I say terrorizing *me*, because I have a feeling they had help."

Behind me, the boys snickered.

"The cedar I kept smelling. You weren't cleansing the house or sending prayers up to Odin. You were covering their scent. You were their accomplice!" I accused.

Energy approached, alerting me so I didn't flinch when a small hand slid into mine. I looked down to see Emil, the youngest and smallest of the three. "We only wanted to bring you some Yule-tide cheer."

The other boys dashed up to my side. "Yeah, we wanted this to be your best Yule ever!" Jon said. He rubbed chocolate from his fingers onto his Thor sweatshirt.

The sound of the travois swishing across the snow ceased as Vidar stopped beside us. He shrugged. "They wanted to do something for you, so we came up with this idea."

I was touched beyond words. Making them all sweat for another moment, I narrowed my gaze at him and shook my head. My façade cracked, a smile breaking through. "Clever boys," I said with a shake of my head.

They burst into laughter.

"I told you she'd like it!" Kris exclaimed.

"Come on!" Emil said, tugging at my hand. "We have gifts for you."

Smiling over the tops of their heads at Vidar, I allowed them to lead me up the steps onto the porch. Vidar and I sat on the porch swing—which the boys had kindly cleared of snow—while they gathered at our feet.

"Here, mine first!" Kris exclaimed as he handed both Vidar and me small packages crudely wrapped in what might have been butcher paper with string tied like ribbon around them.

Some of the wall I had worked for years to build around my heart crumbled. I wasn't used to being given gifts.

We opened them at the same time. Mine was a large smudge stick of spruce, yellow yarrow, and pink heather. It was all bound tightly with jute. Vidar's gift was a small hand broom of straw, jute woven into intricate knots with flowers and crystals adorning it.

Eyes locked on us, eagerly awaiting our reaction, Kris swallowed hard. "I gathered the herbs and branches myself, then my mom showed me how to bind them together. I figured since Vidar used all the smudging he had to cover our scents, you'd need more. And he didn't have a smudging broom. He just waved his hand around, so I figured you'd need a broom too."

I cradled the smudge stick in my lap. "Thank you. It's even more special since you made it yourself," I said softly.

An affirmative grunt came from Vidar. "And this is a handsome broom, very thoughtful of you."

The boy sat up tall, his smile so big it took up half his face. "I purified them with moonlight and asked Frigg to bless them too!"

"They're perfect. Thank you, Kris," Vidar said.

The other two boys began eagerly talking at once, each wanting to go next. Eventually, with some prodding from Kris, Jon let Emil go.

Seeing the three of them laugh, chat, and interact warmed me from the inside. When I'd first me them, Kris and Jon had been bullying Emil. They'd come to my shack of a home to leave me gifts and impress me because I was the uppskera. After I'd had a talk with them about how vital even the least powerful member of a pack was, they'd formed a bond.

It was easily one of the best things that had come from me being the uppskera. These boys and the amazing man at my side made me realize I was much more than the reaper of shifterkind. And there was so much more in my future than just killing. There was life.

After the glossary and cookie recipe you'll find an excerpt of the next novella in the series, Raven Rousting!

THE YULE LADS

Stekkjastaur: He steals sheep's milk

Giljagaur: He loves cow's milk and will steal all of it he can find.

Stúfur: He is a short lad, the shortest of the siblings. He steals leftovers from pans and dishes.

Pvörusleikir: Loves to lick pots clean and will steal unwashed pots to do so.

Askasleikir: Loves to steal bowls, especially those left under beds, and lick them clean.

Hurðaskellir: He slams any open doors.

Skyrgámur: He loves skyr, Icelandic yogurt, and will steal all he can find.

Bjúgnakrækir: He will eat any and all sausages he can find.

Gluggagægir: He's a window peeper, but he's not a creeper, he's looking for things to steal.

Gáttapefur: With his large nose, he sniffs under doorways in search of baked goods.

Ketrókur: This lad loves meat and will steal all of yours, especially lamb chops.

Kertasníkir: This one hordes candles and will steal all those he finds.

GLOSSARY

Hljóð völva: A sound witch.

Hvítur úlfur: A white wolf.

Jólabjór: A brand of Icelandic beer.

Jólabland: Icelandic holiday drink.

Jólabókaflóðið: Flood of books, Icelandic holiday tradition.

Jólakötturinn: Icelandic Christmas cat.

Jötnar: A race of frost giants from Jötunheimr.

Kennari: A teacher.

Mjölnir: Thor's hammer.

Piparkökur: Icelandic holiday cookies similar to ginger snaps.

Sólarsteinn: A sunstone.

Uppskera: Reaper.

Valknut: Triple triangle symbol, some believe it to be the symbol of those loyal to Odin since it also honors the dead who fell in battle.

Varúlfur: A werewolf.

Verða: Becoming.

ENJOY THE READ?

I would be ever so grateful for a review on retail sites (Amazon in particular as reviews there increase a book's visibility, and thereby chances for success, dramatically).

And, I hope you'll continue reading this series in Raven Rousting, the next novella in the Shifter Seeker series. An excerpt of it follows the recipe and glossary.

As a bonus, an excerpt of the first novel in Heather's young adult urban fantasy Channeler series, The Secret of Spruce Knoll, follows after that.

Sonja's *Piparkökur* (Icelandic Pepper Cookies)

2 cups unsweetened applesauce (some like to use 1 ½ cups butter, and ¾ cup corn syrup, but I go for a more unique taste with the applesauce that is much healthier per Detective Sandalius)

1 ¼ cups pure, granulated xylitol (or white sugar if you don't have a Detective Sandalius of your own looking over your shoulder)

½ cup of egg whites (or 2 eggs for a different taste)

3 cups organic flour

1 ½ teaspoons baking powder

1 teaspoon baking soda

½ teaspoon salt

2 teaspoons ground cinnamon

2 teaspoons ground cloves

1 teaspoon ground ginger

¼ teaspoon ground black pepper

*Note: This is the healthy version my friend Elexis Sandalius helped me create (werewolf detective extraordinaire). For a more traditional taste, see the alternative ingredients in the parenthesis.

Preheat oven to 400 degrees. Spray the cookie sheet(s). Mix all dry ingredients. Put all wet ingredients in, mix again until well blended. I'm not big on sifting, no patience for it. But if you feel the urge, go wild.

Use a large spoon to scoop the cookies onto the cookie sheet. Bake for 8-12 minutes (Elevation can make baking time vary quite a bit. Up here at 3500 feet above sea level, I average around 10 minutes). Feed them to the hungry werewolves at your holiday gathering.

RAVEN ROUSTING EXCERPT

Being the werewolf seeker should have come with a manual, but it didn't. At least not one I was allowed access to. Since I wasn't a member of one of the packs of Hemlock Hollow, Montana, I couldn't get into their special library filled with the knowledge of thousands of years of history of our kind. Judgy as hell, if one asked me, which they didn't. So, manual-less and irritated, I trudged through the deep February snow of the forest in search of a newly bitten werewolf left on their own to get through the becoming.

My gut told one was close. They had to be. I only seemed to be able to feel newbies who were on the edge of madness if they were within a mile of me—which sort of felt like a pull deep inside. It was far from an effective locating system. If this really was some sort of Norse God-given ability like so many of my kind thought it was, they needed to work on their power-bestowing details.

No matter which way I went, the pull of the newly bitten didn't get any stronger. But it could be operator error. I wasn't very good at tracking yet. Scents just confused me because now that I was a werewolf there were a million of them, all industrial strength. The snow didn't help matters where that was concerned either.

Once upon a time, I'd had a knack for finding things—animals in particular—while hunting with my dad as a kid. Now, not so much. I was literally stumbling around in the dark, tripping over my own tail at times.

Knowing newly bitten would be drawn to the forest, I'd spent the last week visiting every spot of treed land around where I lived in Missoula, Montana. Rough calluses covered my paws from traipsing about in snow-covered granite hillsides. From the limbs overhead, some sort of bird made a weird "crawk" sound at me as if in mocking agreement of my complete and utter failure. I growled my irritation at it, wishing I knew the wolf equivalent of flipping it off. A snick of my teeth in its direction would have to do. That made two things I should have been innately good at that I sucked at—seeking and werewolf speak. I did not exactly have werewolf skills. In my defense, I'd only been one since last summer.

I'd made it through the becoming—or *verða*, as the citizens of Hemlock Hollow referred to it—only thanks to my hot college professor boyfriend, who was irritatingly good at being a werewolf. Then I'd promptly been abducted, had the power of the seeker forcibly awakened in me, called down lightning on accident, and then been manipulated into opening a portal to one of the other nine worlds along with the werewolf reaper and the guy who bit me. Fail, fail, and epic fail.

Through leafless tree limbs with clumps of snow stuck to them, I spied the three-quarter moon and sighed. I had time. As long as I found the newly bitten—or troubled, as I liked to think of them when they were in this state—before the full moon, I could help them so they didn't lose themselves to the madness of instinct and become a mindless killer. But each hour that ticked by with no sign of them rang in my head like a death bell. If I didn't find them in time and they didn't overcome the draw of the madness, then my best friend the reaper— a.k.a. Ayra Valdisdöttir—stepped in and put them down.

Heedless of my issues, the horizon had grown a lighter shade of blue. The white blanket of frozen crystals that covered everything made the sky that much more brilliant. Daybreak was almost here, which meant any chance of me finding the troubled tonight was over. I needed food and rest. I'd lost track of them anyways. The snow shower that had rolled through covered any tracks they might have left and totally confused scent trails.

Another loud "crawk" from the limbs above startled me, causing me to brace all four legs out, sinking past my wolf ankles in the snow. I looked up and saw a huge black bird peering down at me, head cocked. A crow, or a raven, maybe. I wasn't exactly up on my birds, so it was anyone's guess. It had the stones to make a guttural sound suspiciously similar to laughter. I growled as I extricated myself from the snow and shook it out from between my toes. To my delight, the bird teetered on the branch and nearly fell, catching itself only because it spread its wings and they snagged in the branches.

Shaking my head, I trotted away. At the edge of the forest I located my weatherproof backpack at the base of the huge fir tree I'd hidden it under. Shifting back to human form with the ease of a thought, I quickly dug the huge beach towel out of my pack and wrapped myself in its fluffiness. Today's snow meant the feeling of wet fur stuck with me.

Towel tucked between my breasts, I pulled my worn jeans on. Actual use had made thin spots through the denim and taken it down to threads in areas. It would have been nice if they were an expensive brand that came that way, but no such luck on the salary of a bartender barely keeping her head above student debt thanks to my attempt at a medical degree I'd likely never finish now. Designer clothes were a guilty pleasure of mine, but they had to take a back burner to food and rent.

A blue flash from my phone told me I had a message. I picked it up and checked. It was from Candice, a newly bitten in young woman I'd helped last summer. We'd become fast friends after I hooked her up with a *kennari*—a person who instructs new werewolves.

Candice: *I need a bit of help with something. Can we meet up Wednesday?*

I typed back: *Sure thing. Let me know where and what time.*

To tune out the constant chatter of the clumsy bird, I hummed to myself as I finished dressing, stuffed the towel in my pack, and started out of the forest. The sun was making a spectacular appearance in a pink and purple painted sky when I stepped onto the path leading to the parking lot of the trailhead on the edge of the forest. Two men worked at setting up a camera on a tripod and getting the trailhead just right in the shot. Unfortunately, that put me in the line of sight as well. It was too late to circle around them. My black Jeep sat only three spots from their news van. No doubt they had done that on purpose.

I knew why they were here. It was the same reason I was here—all the animal attacks in the area. And I did not want to talk to them about it. Picking up my pace, I dug my keys out of my jean's pocket. Maybe if I made it before they finished setting up, they wouldn't harass me. One of them spotted me, pointed, and began talking excitedly to the other one about interviewing me. The one with the camera turned it fully in my direction.

Dammit.

"Excuse me, ma'am," the other said as he straightened his peacoat and started my direction.

"You're excused," I mumbled as I stepped off the shoveled path into the snow to go around him. But he followed me quick enough to almost impress a werewolf—certainly quick enough to annoy one.

Brow furrowing, he blinked several times and gaped as if he forgot his next words. I took the opportunity to get a few steps ahead of him without looking supernatural about it. All too quickly, he recovered and dashed to catch up. At this point, I couldn't get away without it being obvious I had inhuman speed. The camera man grabbed the camera off the tripod and followed at a jog. He slipped a few times on the ice, but recovered quickly with telltale Montana native skill.

"Aren't you worried about the amount of reported wolf attacks in the area?" the reporter asked.

"Nope." I kept walking, stepping back onto the cleared path.

A microphone thrust before me. "Really? Why is that?"

Damn, that had been the wrong thing for me to say. Though I wasn't really sure there was a *right* thing to say with the wolf hating media of this area. I wanted to scream that it wasn't the wolves, not to blame them, not to hunt them down and kill them. But if I did that, it opened up an entirely different can of worms.

"No comment," I said instead.

"But, ma'am, you could be attacked by a wolf. That doesn't frighten you?" he asked, now practically running next to me.

The question made me think of the South Fork wolf pack—just normal wolves—my boyfriend told me had been slaughtered due to supposed attacks. Fury erupted through me in the form of words. "No I couldn't, so no it doesn't." Thankfully I retained the good sense to keep my fangs from extending.

The reporter's eyes lit up. "So you don't believe its wolves behind the attacks. What *do* you think it is?"

Double dammit.

Turning a fierce look on him, I rubbed my flannel covered arms. "I think I'm standing out here in only a flannel and jeans, having cooled down from my hike, and now I'm freezing. So if you'll excuse me."

That flummoxed him so much that he gaped like a fish just long enough for me to spin on my boot heals and march away. I speed walked the remainder of the distance to my rattle can black Jeep, by no small miracle making it without slipping and falling on my butt. Using just a touch of supernatural speed, I hopped in, shut the door, and cranked the engine to life with the screwdriver in my console. One day when I was out from under the mountain of student debt I'd accumulated on my journey through med school I would get a new ignition switch installed. Right now I was just happy the heater worked like nobody's business. Before one of the news crew could come to my window, or worse get in the way of me backing out, I slammed it in reverse and got out of there.

Disaster averted, I turned my focus to the next one. I had to find a way to figure out these seeker powers of mine before a newly bitten werewolf who needed my help lost their battle with madness. Unfortunately, that meant swallowing my pride, admitting I didn't know what I was doing, and asking for help. Suddenly I wished facing the media was the worst of my problems.

Continue reading in Raven Rousting, the novella that launches the Shifter Seeker series (spin-off series to the Children of Fenrir series).

ACKNOWLEDGEMENTS

To readers old and new, I cannot thank you enough for reading. You are the blood that keeps my creative heart pumping. Entertaining you brings me so much joy. And to my newfound Booktok community, thank you so much for all your support and encouragement. You people are truly special.

ABOUT THE AUTHOR

When she's not writing, Heather can be found on the slopes, the hiking trails, or paddleboarding. She enjoys the outdoors nearly as much as the worlds she creates. No need to travel to the Great Northwest, though, you can find Heather on social media and her personal site where you can sign up for her newsletter and get access to exclusive content, deals, and giveaways.

http://www.heathermccorkle.com/

WANT SIGNED COPIES?

Check out her site below. Shipping to the continental U.S. is included in the price of all items. If you are outside of the continental U.S. reach out via Heather's Contact Me button on her website and she would be happy to let you know what the shipping cost would be for your delivery. Skol and happy reading!

SIGNED BOOKS:

HEATHER'S WEBSITE:

THE EMERALD WITCHES SERIES (ONGOING):

THE FIRST
RULE OF FAE
KIND IS TO
NEVER
EXPOSE YOUR
MAGIC

IT COULD
GET YOU
LABELED AS A
WITCH, EVEN
IN 1865.

BUT THESE
WOMEN ARE
DONE
FOLLOWING
THE RULES.

THE CHILDREN OF FENRIR SERIES (COMPLETE):

THE CHILDREN OF FENRIR ARE RISING

THE SHIFTER SEEKER SERIES (ONGOING):

CAN THE SEEKER SAVE SHIFTERKIND, OR WILL THEY BE DOOMED TO START RAGNAROK?

GRAB THE SPECIAL EDITION HARDBACKS

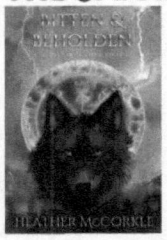

THE SHIFTER SEEKER SERIES (ONGOING):